fans in the stands

Also by Alex Morgan

THE KICKS SERIES

SAVING THE TEAM

SABOTAGE SEASON

WIN OR LOSE

HAT TRICK

SHAKEN UP

SETTLE THE SCORE

UNDER PRESSURE

IN THE ZONE

CHOOSING SIDES

SWITCHING GOALS

HOMECOMING

BREAKAWAY

ALEX MORGAN

Simon & Schuster Books for Young Readers
New York London Toronto Sydney New Delhi

SIMON & SCHUSTER BOOKS FOR YOUNG READERS
An imprint of Simon & Schuster Children's Publishing Division
1230 Avenue of the Americas, New York, New York 10020
This book is a work of fiction. Any references to historical events, real people, or real places are used fictitiously. Other names, characters, places, and events are products of the author's imagination, and any resemblance to actual events or places or persons, living or dead, is entirely coincidental.

Interior design by Krista Vossen
The text for this book was set in Berling.
Manufactured in the United States of America
0221 FFG
First Edition
2 4 6 8 10 9 7 5 3 1

Library of Congress Cataloging-in-Publication Data
Names: Morgan, Alex (Alexandra Patricia), 1989- author.
Title: Fans in the stands / Alex Morgan.
Description: First edition. | New York : Simon & Schuster Books for Young Readers, 2021. | Series: The Kicks | Audience: Ages 8-12. | Audience: Grades 4-6. | Summary: In the weeks leading up to the state championship, Devin and the Kicks have many distractions, including a contest with the boys team to see who can get more fans to watch their games.
Identifiers: LCCN 2020030124 | ISBN 9781534428096 (hardcover) | ISBN 9781534428102 (paperback) | ISBN 9781534428119 (ebook)
Subjects: CYAC: Friendship—Fiction. | Soccer—Fiction. | Contests—Fiction. | Middle schools—Fiction. | Schools—Fiction.
Classification: LCC PZ7.M818 Fan 2021 | DDC [Fic]—dc23
LC record available at https://lccn.loc.gov/2020030124

CHAPTER ONE

"Score! Rose Lavelle scores!" the announcer yelled. We were in Emma's movie room, and I jumped up from the couch, nearly knocking off Zoe, who was right next to me.

"Yes!" I pumped my fist into the air as the other players of the US Women's National Soccer team slapped Rose on the back in congratulations on Emma's practically-movie-screen-size television.

My best friend, Jessi, high-fived me. Some of the other Kicks were also there.

"We're winning!" Jessi crooned. Her hair, which she used to wear in long braids, was a mass of supercute black springy curls that shot out in all directions.

"Yes, but I'm gonna need to switch seats," Zoe chimed in. "Devin, you almost knocked over my drink!"

Zoe was the only one of us wearing a dress, but it was sporty—an off-the-shoulder black Adidas T-shirt dress, with cool white kicks. She was growing out her short hair, and it was starting to curl behind her ears. Zoe was always fashion forward.

"Oops, sorry!" I shrugged. "But you know how excited I get!"

Emma laughed. "I told my mom we should consider putting a tarp over the couches because of what happened last time."

I winced. During the World Cup the previous summer, in my excitement over the US women's team's win, I'd spilled red punch all over my seat. Mrs. Kim, Emma's mom, had been really nice about it, but I had been soooooo embarrassed.

"Don't remind me," I told Emma. She was the tallest of my friends and looked sporty too, with her long black hair pulled back into a ponytail, and a T-shirt with the emblem of the South Korean flag emblazoned in the middle of a soccer ball.

We were watching one of the games in the US Women's National Soccer team victory tour, after they'd won the World Cup. Today was a friendly match with Korea Republic, which was how FIFA, the International Federation of Association Football, referred to the South Korean women's team. Emma and her family were South Korean, and she debated over who to cheer for.

"Since it's a friendly game, I'm going to go ahead and root for Korea," she'd explained nervously when we'd first gotten to her house.

"Oh, don't worry, Devin," Emma said now as she threw an arm around my shoulder. "We'll just have to keep an eye on you. Maybe we should put you in the playroom for a little bit to calm down."

Emma's house was the perfect place to watch the game. It was more like a mansion than a house. The movie room was huge, with sliding glass doors leading out to the backyard, which had an in-ground pool. A large leather sectional surrounded the huge television screen, and there were comfy reclining chairs in place behind it. A long bar along the back wall had tall stools and every kind of soft drink we could imagine, including a new machine that poured out water or seltzer, and ten different fruit flavors we could add to it. Even though I could have had a soda, which I wasn't allowed to have at home, I loved trying all the different-flavored seltzers, so that was usually what I drank when I went to Emma's.

The playroom Emma was referring to was just down the hall from the movie room. It used to be for her and her brothers, but she had a large family with lots of little cousins, so they still used it all the time.

"When the nugget gets bigger, I'll have to bring him," Jessi said. The nugget was Jessi's newborn baby brother, Oliver, who was the cutest baby I'd ever seen. He was so happy and smiley, and almost never cried. Oliver was way different from my little sister, Maisie, who had screamed all the time when she was a baby. Now that she was eight, she could be okay sometimes, but I was glad earbuds had been invented, so I could tune her out when I needed to.

"There's a casting call for babies for a new line of organic baby food," Frida chimed in. "Your mom should take Oliver. He's a natural."

Frida was the only person I'd ever met in person who had been on TV. She was the same age as the rest of us, and played soccer too, but her true passion was acting. She'd been in a bunch of commercials. Her biggest role so far had been in *Mall Mania*, a TV movie that she'd costarred in with the singer Brady McCoy. She'd played his sister. Come to think of it, I guess Frida wasn't the only person I'd met who had been on TV, because she'd gotten Brady to show up for one of our soccer fundraisers, and we'd all gotten to meet him. He was really nice. Emma was a superfan, and I'd thought she was going to pass out, because she completely freaked out when she met him.

"I don't think my mom will go for that," Jessi said.

Frida shrugged. "Not everyone is called to be an actor," she said, a bit dramatically. Frida loved drama, and she loved to stand out, dressing in funky outfits and vintage clothing. Today she was toned down in yoga pants and a T-shirt, her long, reddish-brown hair falling in curls over her shoulders.

"That's true," Jessi said. "Who knows what Oliver will be like when he gets older? All he does now is sleep and eat. And speaking of eating—Emma, that soccer field snack stadium is amazing. And delicious!"

Emma beamed. "My mom and I worked on it all week," she said.

I joined Jessi as she went back to the table next to the bar where the food was set up. Emma and her mom had gone all out and re-created a soccer stadium, filling it with edible goodies.

The field was made out of guacamole, with soft white cheese piped onto it to make the boundary lines, and the goals made out of square pretzels. The back wall of the stadium had cute little American and South Korean flags with toothpick flagpoles.

Carrot sticks with olive heads looked like tiny soccer players on the field. Emma and her mom had cut up empty cereal boxes to make the stands and covered them with white paper and soccer ball stickers. The stands were filled with food: hot dogs, slider burgers, sushi, veggies, dip, potato chips, Cheez Doodles, cookies, candy, fruit, and popcorn. There were so many choices, I almost couldn't decide what to eat.

I filled a paper cup with M&M's and brought them back to the couch so I could snack on them while we watched the rest of the game. As I settled onto the sofa, Jessi sat next to me, with a plate piled high with sushi and potato chips.

"Mmm, sushi," Jessi said.

Zoe moved to the far end of the sectional away from me. "No offense, Devin, but this is a new dress, and I don't want to ruin it."

"It's only M&M's," I protested, holding my cup out and shaking it so she could see. With that, a cascade of the brightly colored candies came pouring out onto my lap.

Everyone started cracking up.

"See? I'm staying right here," Zoe said.

"Oh, Devin," Emma said as I scooped M&M's up from my lap and popped them into my mouth, "you might need to go into the playroom after all."

"I can't help it if you packed so many awesome things into the soccer snack stadium," I said.

"Maybe we can help you make another one, for when the Kicks win the championship," Jessi suggested.

"*If* we win the championship," I said.

"Yeah, don't jinx us, Jessi!" Frida cried.

My friends and I all played soccer for the Kentville Kangaroos, also known as the Kicks. We had made it to the playoffs for our spring season, and we'd won our first two playoff games. First we'd beaten the Victorton Eagles. And this morning we'd faced our longtime rivals, the Rams, on their turf, and had beaten them by just two points. We had only one more game before the final state championship match. It really felt like the win was in our grasp. Now, I wasn't as superstitious as Frida, but I definitely didn't want to spoil our chances either.

"Jessi's not jinxing us," Zoe countered. "We'll practice, we'll play, and we'll either win or lose."

"Thank you for sticking up for me, but don't even say the word *l-o-s-e*," Jessi said. "We're going to win!"

"Shhh," Emma said. "I think the game's coming back on."

But it wasn't the game—it was an ad for the US Men's National Soccer team game coming up next week. As we watched, Frida shook her head.

"It's *ridiculous* that the men get paid more than the women," she said. She'd taken lots of acting classes and knew how to put just the right oomph into anything she said.

I nodded my agreement. "The women's team has an amazing record in the World Cup—better than the men's team does."

"Yeah, they've won, like, four times," Jessi chimed in.

"But when France won the men's World Cup, they got something like thirty-eight million dollars," I said.

Frida tapped her phone screen and gasped. "When the US women's team came in first, they got only four million!"

"Wow, the men got, like—ten times more!" Jessi cried.

Frida fumed. "That's not all. Even in the regular season, the men make about three times as much as the women players. It's totally wrong."

"I heard there's a lawsuit so the players can get equal pay," Zoe commented.

"I hope the women win!" Jessi said. "Remember how the Kicks used to be treated compared to the boys' team? That was awful."

Emma's nodded in agreement. "We didn't even have a real soccer field, just dirt and weeds. We had trash cans as goalposts!"

"And while we were playing on that crummy field, the

boys had a real one to use," I said. "If Sally hadn't paid for ours to get renovated, we'd probably still be playing on dirt with garbage cans."

Sally Lane was the owner of a local sporting goods store. I hadn't thought about her for a while, but the Kicks really owed her a lot. Her confidence in the team had helped us gain more confidence in ourselves, and I definitely know that our playing improved when we weren't stepping into gopher holes. The new field was one of the things that had turned us from a last-place team into contenders for the championship!

"To Sally Lane!" Jessi said, holding a piece of sushi up in the air.

"To Sally Lane!" I said. I raised one of my M&M's to toast by touching it to Jessi's piece of sushi.

Everyone laughed as the game came back on the air. Both teams were good, but in the end, the US won.

"Oh, well." Emma pouted. "Maybe next time."

"Maybe the next World Cup will have South Korea and US in the final," I said, to cheer her up.

"That would be cool!" Emma said.

"And you can make your soccer snack stadium again for us," Jessi replied. "On second thought, I don't want to wait that long."

"It did take a lot of work," Emma said. "I think it will have to be for special occasions only."

I protested. "Hey, every time there's a soccer game is a special occasion."

Jessi laughed. "Soccer-ball-brain Devin."

As we waited for our parents to pick us up, Zoe pulled out her phone to show us her Instagram account.

"I started a new fashion account," she said, a little shyly.

We all oohed and aahed as we pulled out our phones to follow Zoe's new Insta. Her first post featured her oldest sister, Jayne, and was captioned "Working It." It featured Jayne in clothes for her new part-time job, as an office assistant in an accounting firm. She was hoping to be an accountant one day.

"I helped style Jayne for her new job," Zoe explained. "Then we took photos for fun, and Jayne had the idea for me to do a blog and link it to Instagram."

Jayne looked so grown-up and glamorous in the photos, I couldn't believe she was still a senior in high school.

"That's so awesome, Zoe!" I said, proud of my friend. When I had been in Connecticut for another friend's big sweet sixteen party, my luggage had gotten delayed by the airline, along with my party dress. Zoe had saved the day by sending the most beautiful gown at the last minute.

Zoe smiled. "Thanks. I'm really proud of it. I've asked Sabine to do a shoot for me, which would be cool because, besides the fact that she's gorgeous, we still haven't met in person yet. But her schedule's booked for a few weeks."

Sabine and I had met during my very brief modeling career. We'd stayed friends after I'd decided that modeling wasn't for me, and she and Zoe followed each other on social.

"Could you guys help me?" Zoe continued. "I'd interview you about your personal style and take some photos. It'll be really fun and easy, I promise."

Frida was in right away. "Of course!"

Jessi smiled and said, "Sure, why not? Although, I know I'm not as *gorgeous* as Sabine."

Zoe blushed. "You definitely are! But you know what I mean. Sabine is . . ."

"Stunning!" Frida finished for her. "But I'm not intimidated. I know how to make the camera fall in love with me."

"I'll do it," I said, but I was still thinking about Zoe's blush. Was she crushing on Sabine? If she was, that would make perfect sense. They had so much in common. I was about to ask her, when Emma spoke up.

"I wear jeans and T-shirts every day. It's like my uniform," she said. "I'm way too casual to be on a fashion blog."

Zoe shook her head. "You've got a great look, Emma, and I'll take care of helping you pick out what to wear. It'll be painless, I promise."

Easygoing Emma agreed. "Okay, you talked me into it!"

As our parents' cars started to arrive and we said goodbye, I reflected on how lucky I was to have such great friends. When I'd first come to California after moving from Connecticut, I had been really homesick. Then I'd met the Kicks, and everything had changed.

CHAPTER TWO

The final bell rang, signaling the end of Monday's classes, and I jumped out of my seat, along with the other kids in my class. We spilled into the hallway of Kentville Middle School, where everyone was talking loudly and running around, whooping noisily.

Everyone seemed more energetic than usual, and I guessed it had something to do with spring. Even though we didn't feel the seasons in California like I had when I'd been in Connecticut, something happened toward the end of the school year. Summer break was almost here, and each day it got a little bit harder to concentrate in class.

I was thinking about this when Steven bumped into me—actually, *literally* bumped into me because Cody was chasing him.

"Sorry, Devin," he said.

"No problem," I said. "You guys going to practice?"

"Yeah," he replied, running his hand through his black, spiky hair. Then he grinned. "I can't believe we're both in the playoffs! So cool, right?"

I nodded. "It would be awesome if the Kicks and the Kangaroos both won their championships."

"I think we can do it," Steven said. He nodded. "Gotta go. See you!"

He ran off, and I got kind of a warm, fuzzy feeling, watching him leave. I guess if I had a crush on anybody, it was Steven. And I knew he liked me, too, which was very cool. Sometimes me and Steven and Jessi and Cody hung out together, and it was a lot of fun. And when the school had dances and things, we went together. I thought I was too young to have a boyfriend, but sometimes I daydreamed about being Steven's girlfriend. Going to high school dances, prom, driving around in a car together, stuff like that.

Better get moving, I told myself, and I ran to the girls' locker room to change for practice. My teammates were there, all quickly getting dressed in shorts and blue-and-white practice shirts. Then we grabbed our backpacks and headed out to the girls' practice field, where the Kicks played.

The main field, where the boys got to practice, was still on school grounds. There were metal bleachers, and a digital scoreboard, and perfectly maintained green grass lined with crisp white stripes.

To get to the girls' field, you had to walk across the street to the community park. When I'd first joined the Kicks in the fall, the field had been a muddy mess, with brown grass and trash-can goalposts. The field had made practice a lot harder than it should've been. That was why we had toasted Sally Lane on Saturday—thanks to her, we now had real goalposts. We also had landscaping, all of the soccer balls we needed, and even a small section of bleachers.

When we got there, one of my teammates, Megan, ran to the bag of soccer balls and pulled one out. She tossed it to Grace, my co-captain.

"Come on, Grace, show everybody!" Megan urged.

"I still don't have it down yet," Grace protested.

"I know you can do it!" Megan said.

Curious, we all gathered around Grace. She began dribbling the ball between her feet. Then, swiftly, she moved it outside her right foot and tried to kick it up behind her and over her head. I had seen pro players do that move, but I'd never tried it myself. Grace's attempt sent the ball careening away to her right.

She frowned. "I told you I don't have it down," she said to Megan.

But Megan wouldn't let her give up. She tossed Grace a new ball. "I've seen you do it. Come on!"

Grace screwed up her face in concentration. She dribbled, then kicked the ball up behind her with her heel. This time the ball went straight up and over Grace's head. She hopped back a little bit to get the ball in front of her, and kicked it to Emma, who caught it.

Everybody clapped and cheered, and Grace grinned.

"That was awesome!" Jessi cried.

"I've been practicing it since I saw it," Grace said. "I don't think I'd ever use it on the field, but it's fun to do."

"Do the pros really do that during a match?" Zoe asked.

"Sometimes," Grace answered. "It's a way to confuse your defender if you're not fast enough to get past them."

Jessi ran to get another ball. "I want to try!"

While a few other girls followed her and began trying the move, sending balls rocketing across the field, Coach Flores approached me and Grace.

"Grace, Devin, why don't you lead the team in a drill?" she asked. "You've both worked so hard this season, and you're great leaders."

"Sure thing, Coach," Grace replied. "Anything you want us to do?"

"Your choice," Coach said, and then she moved over to the bleachers, where she stood and watched.

I looked at Grace. "What do you want to do?"

Grace looked over at the players trying to do the pro move. "Well, maybe not *this.* But have you ever heard of a step-over?"

I nodded. "It's a move used to fake out a defender. I'm not sure if everyone else on the team knows how to do it, though."

"I learned it at soccer camp," Grace said. "Might as

well have everyone try it, right? It'll be fun."

We jogged toward the others, and Grace clapped her hands. She's pretty quiet, normally, but when she's leading the team, she can get loud.

"Okay, everybody, line up!" she called out, and my teammates quickly moved into a single line, facing us.

"We're going to learn what may be a new move to some of you today," Grace said. "For the rest of you, we can work on practicing and perfecting it. There are a few other things you can do to confuse a defender besides kick the ball over your own head. You can change your speed. You can feint, which means you pretend you're going to go one way, but you go the opposite way instead. This move—it's called a step-over, or a scissor—is a kind of feint."

I watched Grace, impressed. She was a year older than I was, in eighth grade, and she loved soccer as much as I did.

Grace nodded at me, and I faced her in an opposing position. She dribbled the ball with the outside of her right foot, moving her body so it looked like she was going to go right. Then she stepped over the ball completely with her right foot. When her foot hit the ground, she got control of the ball with the outside of her left foot, kicking it into the open space—and away from me.

"Did you see that?" she asked. She grabbed another ball and demonstrated again. "It's important to remember to dribble with the *outside* of your foot. Step over the ball. Then kick it away with the outside of your other foot."

I chimed in. "Everybody, pair up. Take turns defending and trying the move."

The field got quiet as everyone concentrated on the drill. I stayed paired with Grace and, since I had done it before, figured it would be easy. Yet the first time, I hit the top of the ball with my foot when I tried to do the step-over, and stumbled. But the second time, I got it right. It was a tricky move, and I'm glad Grace thought of getting the team together to practice it.

"Nice!" Grace congratulated me.

I looked around at my teammates, and everybody was getting the hang of it. Even Emma, who was much better tending goal than she was with footwork, was managing to step over the ball without tripping.

"Nice way to stay on your feet, Emma!" I yelled, encouraging her.

As soon as I said that, Frida slipped and knee-planted in the grass. Jessi, her partner, reached out a hand to her, and I ran over.

"You okay?" I asked.

"Just a scrape," she said, and I noticed that her knee was bleeding.

"Let me get the first aid kit," I said, and I jogged over to the bleachers to get the first aid kit from Coach, with Jessi at my heels. We found Coach talking to a young woman carrying a spiral notebook.

"I do believe that women soccer professionals should get paid the same as men," Coach was saying. "It's not even about who's more popular. The women's games bring in the same amount of TV viewers."

"That's exactly why they should get paid the same!" Jessi chimed in loudly.

The woman laughed. "Coach Flores, would you mind if I talked to some of your players?"

"That's fine with me, if they don't mind. You'll just have to contact their parents if you want to publish their names," Coach replied. "Is that why you girls came over?"

"Actually, Frida hurt her knee," I said. "Just a scrape."

Coach nodded and turned to the reporter. "Give us a minute, Emily."

We followed Coach Flores out onto the field and watched while she cleaned and bandaged Frida's knee. Then the team continued the drill and Coach brought Jessi and me back to the reporter.

"This is Emily Kratzer, from the *Kentville Chronicle*," Coach Flores explained. "She's doing an article about why professional women's soccer players don't get paid as much as men."

"We were *just* talking about that the other day!" Jessi said. "It's so unfair."

"First, let me get your names and ages," Emily said, and she jotted them down as we gave them to her. "Jessi, you seem to have a pretty strong opinion on the subject of women soccer pros getting paid the same as men. Why do you feel that way?" she asked.

"It's like Coach said," Jessi said. "The women are just

as popular. And they win more than the guys do!"

"What do you think, Devin?" Emily asked me.

"Well, boys' sports always get more funding and attention," I said. "Before Sally Lane fixed it up, the girls' practice field was a real mess. But the boys' field is perfect!"

"Sally Lane? Of Lane's Sporting Goods?" Emily asked. "I think I remember that story."

I nodded. "Yeah, she really helped us out," I said. "But I mean, why was that field the boys' field in the first place? Why didn't we take turns or something? It seems like people think that boys are better at sports. Which isn't always true."

Emily asked more questions, and she took notes while Jessi and I talked. It felt good to have someone else hear our opinions outside of Emma's movie room.

"Will this really be in the newspaper?" Jessi asked.

"I need to get your parents' contact info from Coach Flores, and if they're okay with me interviewing you, this should be in Wednesday's paper," she told us.

"Cool!" Jessi said.

"Thanks," I told her. "We'd better get back to practice."

Emily thanked us, and Jessi and I joined our teammates, along with Coach.

"All right, girls," she said. "We've got one last playoff game this coming Saturday. If we win that, we'll go to the championship. Are we ready?"

"Ready, Coach!" we shouted back.

Coach grinned. "I can't hear you!"

"READY, COACH!"

Coach clapped her hands. "That's the spirit! Now let's get out there and scrimmage!"

My heart was pumping as we jogged out onto the field. The championship was within reach, and I could almost taste it!

CHAPTER THREE

When my phone alarm went off Wednesday morning, I sprang out of bed.

Sometimes I hit snooze if I was feeling extra tired, but today was different. Being in the middle of playoff season meant I needed to get extra training in, so I was wide awake. Some mornings I went for a jog, but today I wanted to focus on stretches and exercises that would prevent injury. One of my worst fears was getting sidelined during a playoff game because I got hurt. I decided I would do my best to keep that from happening!

I went to the wall in my bedroom and did some simple calf raises to ward off shin splints, which is when the large bone in the front of your lower leg—the tibia—gets stressed from too much activity. The condition can be really painful, and it has benched plenty of athletes. I leaned forward against the wall with both hands and raised my heels until I was on my tippy-toes. I held that position for a few seconds, then released, and repeated the motion several times.

After that I moved on to standing calf stretches, keeping my hands on the wall but extending one leg back, heel down, until I could feel the gentle pull on the muscle. I switched legs several times until my calves felt warm and loose. I moved into some stretches of my quadriceps—the big muscle in the front of the thigh—this time away from the wall. Balancing on my left foot, I placed my hand above my right ankle and pulled my right leg back at the knee. Then I switched legs back and forth, and after that I did some arm and shoulder stretches.

It wasn't a big workout, but I had a more serious one planned for that afternoon. We didn't usually have soccer practice on Wednesdays, so Jessi and I were getting together at my house after school to run some drills.

I took a quick shower and hurriedly put on a short-sleeved crew-neck knit dress with light-blue and white stripes. I paired it with navy sneakers. My brief time as a model for teen activewear had exposed me to some cute, sporty looks. I'd added new pieces to my wardrobe, all thanks to a fun shopping trip I'd taken with my mom.

I checked my phone, and there was a text and pic from Kara, my friend from Connecticut. Whenever we could, we texted each other a picture of what we were wearing to school that day. We used to do it every day when I first moved to California, but after a few months, we'd each gotten busy with our lives. I hadn't thought that was a big deal, but on a recent visit to Connecticut, I'd learned that Kara thought I'd changed since I'd moved to California—and I thought that Kara was different now too. We got into kind of a big fight over it, but we ended up talking it out. No matter what, Kara would always be one of my best friends.

From the picture Kara had sent me, I could tell it was still cold in Connecticut, even though it was spring. Her pink baby-doll sweaterdress, gray tights, gray scarf, and tan booties told the tale.

U look fab! I texted her, and then I took a quick pic in my full-length mirror to send back to her. Look! No flip-flops!

When I'd first moved to Cali, I'd lived in my flip-flops 24/7, except of course on the soccer field! Now it was fun to mix it up a bit.

My stomach rumbled as I sniffed the air. I smelled bacon! I hurried down the stairs and into our kitchen. I barely glanced at my parents, who were huddled together at the table, sharing the newspaper they both seemed to be reading at once.

My focus instead was on the platter on the counter, piled high with turkey bacon, scrambled eggs, and whole-grain toast.

"Yum!" I said, filling my plate. Most mornings we had quick oats and fruit, or something else fast and easy. This was a real weekday-morning treat.

I sat down at the kitchen table, and that was when I noticed that both of my parents were completely quiet, just staring at me and smiling.

"Uh, good morning?" I said, a little confused. Maisie was eating on the couch while she watched cartoons, which was usually not allowed, so she was either being rewarded for doing something good or being bribed into doing something she didn't want to.

"Oh, Devin, I am just so proud of you," my mom said, and it looked like her eyes were filled with tears.

I started to get worried. "What's wrong?" I asked.

My dad laughed as my mom dabbed at her eyes with a napkin. "Nothing, Devin. It's the opposite of wrong. We just read the article you were interviewed for in the *Kentville Chronicle*," he said.

"Oh, right! The reporter said the article would be printed today," I said, remembering. "How did it come out? What does it say?" I leaned eagerly toward the paper.

My dad cleared his throat and began reading:

"'Even though they haven't won a state championship since the 1990s, the Kentville "Kicks" middle school girls soccer team is knocking on the door this season for a regional championship win that will put them in sight of a state victory.'"

I liked the sound of that!

"'While emphasis is mostly on practice and play,'" Dad continued reading, "'the Kicks are also thinking about a controversy that has the entire world talking: equal pay for women's and men's professional soccer teams.

"''I do believe that women soccer professionals should get paid the same as men," Coach Flores of the Kicks said. "It's not even about who's more popular. The women's games bring in the same amount of TV viewers."

"'Kentville Kicks player Jessi Dukes, thirteen, agreed enthusiastically with her coach.

"''They should get paid the same!" she said. "The women are just as popular. And they win more than the guys do."

"'Her teammate Devin Burke, twelve, shared that the Kicks have had personal experience with inequality on the soccer field.

"''Well, boys' sports always get more funding and attention," said Burke. "Before Sally Lane fixed it up, the girls' practice field was a real mess. But the boys' field is perfect!"

"'Sally Lane of Lane's Sporting Goods confirmed the sorry state the girls' field used to be in. "More dirt and weeds than grass, and the poor girls didn't even have goal posts. They had to use trash cans instead! When I saw a game one day, I was horrified at the conditions of their soccer field and wanted to help. So I did."

"'While Burke and Dukes are both grateful to Lane, they do wonder why an outsider had to intervene.

"''She really helped us out," Burke said. "But . . . why was that field the boys' field in the first place? Why didn't we take turns or something?"'"

As Dad continued reading out loud all the things that Coach, Jessi, and I said to the reporter at practice that day, I couldn't help but feel proud and important. Like people would read what I had to say and maybe change their minds about women athletes.

Dad continued reading: "'When Principal Gallegos of Kentville Middle School was asked about the soccer field disparity, he said in an email, "It was purely a budget and scheduling issue. Both the boys and girls teams at Kentville get all the support and help we can give them."'"

The article went on to talk more about the pay gap in professional soccer, a lawsuit around that, and how some private companies donated money to the women's national team to help make up the pay difference, but I couldn't stop thinking of how proud I was about what Coach, Jessi, and I had said. I couldn't believe it was in the paper!

"We are so proud to have a daughter who can speak on important subjects so eloquently, Devin," my mom said, covering my hand with her own and giving it a squeeze.

"You did good, kid." My dad winked at me as he slid an extra piece of bacon onto my plate.

Suddenly I had a thought that made my heart stop for a second. "Wait! Do you think Principal Gallegos will be mad at me?"

My mom shook her head. "You only told the truth and asked a question that everyone was thinking. If he's angry about that, he'll have to deal with me." And she got up and gave me a big hug.

When I got to school that day, I was in a great mood. I knew that I was just a middle school student from a small town, but maybe what I'd said would make some people think.

News must have spread, because as I walked into the building, several people stopped me to say they liked the article.

"Nicely done, Devin," Vice Principal Vazquez said as she walked by me. That made me feel a whole lot better. If the vice principal wasn't angry, then I probably wasn't in any trouble.

"We're famous!" Jessi said, running up to me in the hall before first period. "And Coach, too!"

"It's so cool," I told her.

"Now they'll have to raise the women's team's pay, because we said so." Jessi grinned. "I'll see you at lunch. I brought a copy of the newspaper. We can read it again!"

I kept getting compliments from my classmates. I hadn't thought any kids my age read the paper, but apparently the article was online, and people were sharing the link.

Then, on the way to World Civ, I met Steven in the hallway. He and I always walked to class together.

"Hey," I said, and waited for him to mention the article.

But he just said "Hey" in return and that was it, until Anna, one of my fellow Kicks, walked by and said, "Great article, Devin!"

I smiled shyly at Steven, glad someone else had brought it up. "Yeah, I was in the paper," I told him.

"I heard about it," Steven said, to my surprise. "Cody sent me the link. I get where you're coming from, but I don't totally agree with you."

Huh? What? My mind kind of went blank for a moment. What was there not to agree about?

"Really?" I asked, trying to keep my voice low and calm. "In what way?"

"Well, you left out some important stuff. Like the fact that the men only get paid if they play. But on the women's team, they get paid even if they're sitting out a game. They've got it better."

"How is it better if the men get paid way more to begin with?" I asked.

"The men deserve it, since they bring in more fans," Steven said.

I was stunned. "How do you know that? That's not what I heard."

Steven tried to defend his argument. "They bring more fans into the stadiums. It's a fact," he insisted, his cheeks turning a little red. "And they get way more advertising money."

"Maybe they get more companies to sponsor them just because they're men, and people think men are better athletes than women," I countered.

"Well, I mean, there's a reason why men and women don't play against each other," he said. "You know, because guys are stronger and stuff."

"Seriously?" I asked. "If we both turn pro, do you think you deserve to make more money than me just because you're a boy?"

"I didn't say that—" Steven began, but I cut him off.

"I think I can find my own way to World Civ. I don't need a *boy* to show me," I said over my shoulder as I stalked down the hall and away from him as fast as my legs could carry me.

As I slid into my seat in the classroom, I noticed I was shaking a bit. I took a deep breath to calm myself, but it was tough. I'd never expected to have an argument with Steven about something like this.

This isn't the Steven I know, I thought. *But what if I really don't know Steven at all?*

CHAPTER FOUR

Reading about ancient China that morning helped me forget about my argument with Steven for a little while. But when lunchtime came, I really wanted to talk about things with my friends.

One thing that was different about going to school in California and going to school in Connecticut was that in Cali you could eat lunch outside. My friends and I usually ate at a table under a shady potted palm tree, and when I got there, I found Jessi, Emma, and Frida gathered around Zoe.

"What's going on?" I asked, and Zoe held out her phone.

"I posted my first fashion photos today," she announced. I looked at the screen, and there was a cute photo of Zoe, next to the title *Fashion from A to Zoe.*

"Cool! If anyone knows fashion from *A* to *Z*, it's you," I said. "How do I subscribe?"

"I'll post the pictures on Insta, so you can just click through from there," she answered.

We were all quiet as we scrolled through the photos she'd taken. There was an auburn-haired girl with a red rose in her hair that matched her vintage-looking red dress.

"Is that—Frida?" I asked.

Frida grinned. "Isn't it awesome? We did the shoot on Sunday in Zoe's backyard. I brought some of my own clothes, and Zoe gave me some clothes she had, and she accessorized everything."

"Who did your makeup?" Emma asked. "You look gorgeous!"

"Yvette did it," Frida replied, mentioning one of Zoe's sisters.

"I had to beg her, because she has her own makeup blog, and she's convinced she's a social media superstar," Zoe said. "But she did a great job."

I looked back at the post. Zoe had titled it "Looks for a Dramatic Diva," and she had written a bunch of tips for how to dress like the "diva inside you." Stuff like *Don't be afraid of bold colors* and *Choose oversize accessories, like belts and sunglasses, for a look your fans will always remember*.

The photos were really amazing. There was one of Frida in a yellow dress and large black sunglasses, gazing up at the sun; another of Frida in jeans, a white button-down shirt, a wide belt, and a statement necklace, picking a flower in Zoe's garden; and another of Frida twirling around in a black sparkly skirt and chunky heels.

We all started talking at once.

"This literally looks like a fashion magazine!" Jessi said.

"It's really good," I agreed.

Emma turned to Frida. "You should be an actress *and* a model."

"I'd prefer to stick to studying acting," Frida said. "It's a *craft*. Not just standing around looking pretty. No offense, Devin."

"That's okay," I said, and I meant it, because that was just Frida being the dramatic diva that she was. "I'm not even modeling anymore. But it was a lot harder than just standing around. It takes skill. That's why I quit. I just wasn't that good at it."

"But you'll come out of retirement for my blog, right?" Zoe asked. "I'm shooting Emma next, and then I need to shoot you and Jessi."

"What will your theme for mine be?" Emma asked. "Cuddly Klutz? Silly Slob? Gawky and Goofy?"

Zoe hugged her. "You are way too hard on yourself! I've got the perfect idea for your shoot. Just trust me. It's going to be amazing."

Emma hugged her back. "Only you could get me to model, Zoe. Only you."

Then we dug into our lunches.

"I'm glad you're willing to do my blog, Devin, considering you're a superstar now," Zoe teased. "Everyone's talking about that newspaper article."

That reminded me. "Yeah, Steven talked to me about it, and I wasn't too happy with what he said," I blurted out.

My friends looked shocked.

"Sweet Steven?" Emma asked. "What did he say?"

"He told me he thinks the male soccer players *should* get paid more than the women. He even said that men are stronger and better players!" I said.

Jessi pounded her hand on the table. "He did *not*!"

I nodded. "He did. And I don't know what to do with that. It seems so obvious to me that the women players should get paid the same as the men. So what does that say about the kind of person Steven is?"

"Well, you know, he's always been nice to you, Devin," Emma said slowly. "I mean, this is just one thing."

"I know," I said. "But to me it kind of feels like a *big* thing."

Frida turned to Jessi. "What would you do if Cody said something like that?"

"Cody wouldn't say something like that," Jessi replied.

"Are you sure?" I asked her.

"There's one way to find out," Jessi said, and she jumped up.

"Oh boy," I said, and I followed her. Zoe, Emma, and Frida came too.

Jessi walked across the courtyard and planted her hands on the boys' lunch table. Cody and Steven were sitting with some other guys from their soccer team.

"Hey, Jessi!" Cody said, brushing a strand of wavy blond hair from his eyes.

"Hey," Jessi said. "I'm just wondering. Steven here says that it's okay that the men's pro soccer team gets paid more than the women's team. What do you think?"

Cody shrugged. "Sure," he said. "They're more popular. And they're better players."

"That's not true!" I piped up. "If they were better players, maybe they would win a World Cup once in a while!"

"This is a dumb argument," Steven said. "It's not important."

"Of course it's important!" Jessi shot back. "What if some of us go on to become pro players?"

"The women still get paid a lot of money," Cody argued.

"Like I said before, Devin, it's because the men get more advertisers," Steven added.

"But why should they, if they're not winning games? Or getting as many viewers?" I asked.

By now we were getting loud, and a few kids had come over to listen, including Grace and Megan.

"Do you really think not paying women the same is okay?" Megan asked.

"I'm not saying it's *okay*. I'm just saying it makes sense," Steven said.

Megan rolled her eyes. "Of course you'd say that. You're a boy."

A voice behind me joined in. "Not all boys think that way."

I turned to see Foley, a boy from my algebra class.

"The women's team deserves equal pay," Foley said. "Especially because of their winning record."

"Exactly!" Jessi cried, slamming her hands down onto the boys' lunch table again.

"Whoa. Calm down, Jessi!" Cody said.

Uh-oh, I thought. *That wasn't a smart move*.

"Do NOT tell me to calm down!" Jessi said loudly.

My mind was racing. There had to be some way to settle this. Some way to prove our point.

Then it hit me.

"Hold on," I said. "Maybe we should settle this on the field."

"You mean like a girls versus boys game?" Cody asked. "We'd totally beat you."

"That's debatable, but that's not what I'm saying," I said. "The argument is really about popularity, right? Because if a team is popular, they get more sponsors and stuff. So maybe we should see who brings more fans to the stands."

"How would we do that?" Steven asked.

"I get it!" Jessi cried. "We each have at least one more playoff game, right? So we can see which team gets more fans at their match."

"That's no contest," Cody said. "We'd still win."

"Don't be so sure," Jessi snapped.

"Wait, how would we count the fans? How would we make sure it's fair?" Steven asked.

Foley spoke up again. "Maybe you could get volunteers

to count the fans. Like from the student council or something. I'd do it."

I looked at Foley and smiled. "Thanks," I said.

I could swear he blushed, and I didn't know why. But it made me notice the freckles across his cheeks, which were kind of cute.

Then Steven stood up and held out his hand to me.

"You're on," he said. "Let's see who can get more fans in the stands at the next playoff game."

"Fine," I said, and we shook hands.

That was a signal for all of us to go back to our tables. Grace and Megan followed us.

"You know, Devin, we really should make sure the rest of the team is cool with this," Grace told me.

"I didn't even think of that!" I said. "Sorry."

"Don't be sorry," Grace said. "It's a good idea. Maybe the only way to make a point to the boys. I'll start a group chat and see what everyone thinks."

"It'll be awesome if we win," Megan said. "But what if we don't? We'll never hear the end of it."

We all got quiet, even Jessi. That thought hadn't occurred to me when I'd brought up the idea. But if the boys won, they would make our lives unbearable!

"Then we can't lose," I said, trying to sound more confident than I was. "We'll get people in the stands. We'll win the championship. We'll show the boys that we're right!"

Chapter Five

"Girls against the boys?" Mom repeated that night at dinner when I told her what had happened at lunchtime. "I'm not sure how I feel about that."

"What do you mean?" I asked. That wasn't the reaction I'd been hoping for.

"Well, equality between men and women is the kind of argument you can win with facts and logic," Mom said. "And I'm not sure if this contest is such a smart idea. If you lose, the boys will think they made a point. But you can't really compare this to professional sports."

Dad chimed in. "I think it sounds like a fun way to explore the issue," he said. "And it'll be good to bring a lot of energy to the games, regardless."

"I'll help you beat those boys!" Maisie said, agreeing with me—something she never did. But I think, at eight years old, she disliked boys more than she disliked me.

"I'll invite all my friends to your game on Saturday!"

"Thanks, Maisie," I said, but I picked at the salmon on my plate nervously. Mom had a point—using facts and logic was a better way to win an argument than having a contest. And if we lost, it could really hurt what we were trying to say.

Why did I open my mouth? I worried. I should have let the argument drop!

Dad noticed the look on my face. "Don't worry, Devin," he said. "A little competition is a healthy thing, and I think it's going to be fun for all of you. And if I know you and your friends, you'll find a way to win."

"Thanks, Dad," I said, and I began eating again.

Before I checked in with Kara after dinner, I looked at the group chat with the other Kicks. My mom had made a good point. What did the others think? I was relieved to read that the majority of the Kicks were ready to take on the challenge and were pretty confident we'd beat the boys.

"Let's crush them!" Taylor wrote.

"No worries, I've got a BIG family," Giselle said.

Then I spoke with Kara, and she made me feel even better.

"You are so going to beat those boys," she said. "For one thing, girls are much more organized."

"Really?" I asked, looking around at my messy room, which at that moment looked like it had been decorated with old sweat socks.

"Definitely," Kara said. "I bet you'll come up with way better ideas to get the fans there than the boys will."

"Right. Ideas," I said. Actually, I hadn't thought of any ideas yet. "Um, what kind of ideas?"

Kara was quiet for a minute. "The skies are always clear in California, right? Maybe you could chip in and hire a skywriter? Or a plane with one of those banners behind it, like we used to see when we went down the shore."

"Wow," I said. "That would be amazing." *And hard to do!* I thought.

"You'll think of something, Devin," Kara assured me. "I'm rooting for you! If I could fly out to your game, you know I would."

"Thanks," I said. On the one hand, she'd given me confidence. On the other hand, I worried about disappointing her!

I texted Grace. Should we maybe start to plan ways to get people to our game?

Was just about to text you, she said. Let's call for a meeting after practice tomorrow.

Great! I replied, and soon a flurry of texts went back and forth in the Kicks group chat. Before I fell asleep, we had plans to meet at a diner, and parents who had volunteered to drive. That helped boost my confidence again.

A lot of people seem to believe in this, I thought. *Maybe it isn't such a bad idea after all!*

• • •

The contest with the boys was on my mind the next morning as I walked into algebra. Before the bell rang, Foley came up to my desk.

"Hey, Devin," he said, a little shyly.

"Hey," I replied.

He cleared his throat. "So, um, I was thinking about what you said yesterday, and I talked to the members of the math team, and they agreed to go to both games this weekend to calculate the number of fans."

"Wow, that's awesome," I said. "Thanks!"

He put a piece of paper on my desk. "We talked about the best way to do it, and we thought we should try to count only the fans who come to root for Kentville, because the other school might have their own way of attracting fans to the games, so counting them would skew the results."

I nodded. "That makes sense."

"We're thinking we can post ourselves at the gate and count the fans who walk in the direction of the Kentville stands," Foley went on. "It won't be one-hundred-percent accurate, but it will be close."

I glanced at the report, which had percentages on it and even a graph. "This is amazing," I said. "I'll show it to the Kicks and to the boys' team too, but I'm sure everyone will think it's fair."

"Great!" Foley said.

The bell rang, and Foley turned to go to his seat. Then he looked back.

"I know it's not scientific to have a preference, but I hope the Kicks win," he said.

I grinned at him. "Me too," I said, and I swear he blushed again.

Cute freckles, I thought, and then I blushed too. I had barely ever talked to Foley before. And suddenly I thought he was cute, just because he agreed with me?

I still like Steven, I told myself. *Once this contest is over, things will be back to the way they were!*

"Fries with cheese," Jessi told the waiter. "Extra cheese."

We were seated at a very long table in the Palm Tree Diner, ordering our food. It was an enormous restaurant with a sit-down counter at the front and big tables in the back, where we were. Our table faced a huge wall mural of surfers on a sandy beach.

Before she'd said I could go, Mom had looked over the menu online and given me just enough money for my order and a tip.

"One salad with grilled chicken and a lemonade," I told the waiter, handing them my menu.

"Don't worry. You can share my fries," Jessi told me.

"Thanks!" I said.

I gazed around the table at everyone who'd been able to come to the diner. Grace, Megan, Anjali, Giselle, Taylor, and Jade were clustered at one end, with me, Jessi, Zoe, Frida, Emma, Hailey, and Brianna at the other. Once the waiter took all the orders, Grace spoke up.

"Okay, so we're here to figure out how to get fans to our game on Saturday. And that's only two days away, so we need to act fast. Does anybody have any ideas?" she asked.

Everybody kind of looked at one another for a second, so I raised my hand.

"My friend Kara said we should chip in for a skywriter," I offered, but it sounded silly as soon as I said it. "But I guess that's kind of complicated."

"What if we do a giveaway, like they do at big stadiums?" Hailey piped up. "You know, like a bobblehead, or a water bottle, or something like that."

"That's an awesome idea, but it would cost money, just like the skywriter," Grace pointed out. "We need to think of something free."

"We could hold a bake sale or something to raise the money," Emma suggested.

Grace frowned. "We could, but we only have two days."

"What if we all ask ten people we know to come?" Giselle suggested. "You know, like our relatives, maybe."

I nodded. "That would be a good start. But maybe not everybody knows ten people who could come." I was one of them. We didn't have any relatives at all in California, although maybe Dad could ask his coworkers—but would that be weird? What kind of adults would want to come to a middle school soccer game?

Frida raised her hand. "I think we need to use the power of social media," she said. "We could create a campaign."

Zoe spoke up. "Maybe we could ask kids from other schools who we know," she said. "Like, I could ask Sabine, and maybe she could ask other kids she knows to come."

"Sure," Grace said. Then she repeated what I had just been wondering. "It couldn't hurt. But it might be hard to get people who don't even know us to come watch us play."

The waiter—an older man with a friendly smile—came back with a tray full of drinks. Another server, a young woman with blue streaks in her hair, carried another tray.

Jessi read their name tags. "Scott, Lauren, can we ask you something?"

"Sure," Scott said, placing my lemonade in front of me, and Lauren shrugged.

"Would you ever go to see a girls' soccer game?" Jessi asked.

"I might, if my niece were playing," Scott answered.

Lauren shook her head. "Sorry, I don't like sports."

"But what if you knew that the girls were playing to prove something?" Jessi said. "For example, if they had a bet going with a boys' team that the girls could get more fans, to prove that women soccer players should get paid as much as men?"

Scott smiled. "Is that what you all are doing?"

"Well, it's not a bet, exactly," I responded. "We're just hoping we can get the boys to see the truth."

"Well, then I might go, if I knew about it," Scott answered. "I read all about the women's soccer team getting paid so much less than the men's. That's really not fair."

He looked at Lauren.

"*Maybe* I would go," she said. "Soccer is boring, but equal pay is important."

"Yes!" Jessi cheered.

"We'll be back soon with your food," Scott said, and he and Lauren left.

Frida was scrolling on her phone. "We should hashtag 'Kentville Middle School,' 'girls' soccer,' and 'Kentville,' and we should also try the 'Equal Pay' hashtag that everyone who supports the US women's team is using."

"Perfect!" Grace said. "That would reach people like Lauren and Scott, maybe."

"I can create some posts, and everyone can share them," Frida suggested.

"I also think we should make flyers," Giselle said. "I can create some with my art program tonight and email everybody. We can print them out and bring them to school in the morning and put them up."

"Do we need permission to do that?" Grace asked.

"I don't think so," Megan said. "It's like school spirit, right?"

"Are you going to mention the girls-versus-boys thing on the flyers? And in the posts?" I asked. "Or is this just about getting people to the games?"

Everyone was quiet while we thought about the best

way to do the publicity. Scott and Lauren came with our food, and we started eating.

After a few minutes Frida spoke up. "Maybe the flyers for school could just have the time and place of the game, and ask for people to come out," she suggested. "And on social media I could say something like, 'Help us prove that girls' sports are just as popular as boys' sports.'"

"That sounds good," Grace said. "And I think we should all still try to invite ten people to come, like Giselle said."

"We might as well do everything we can," I said. "I really don't want to lose to the boys."

"Everything's going to work out, Devin," Jessi said. "Here, have a cheese fry."

"Okay," I said, taking the fry from her. "I am going to print out *so* many flyers when I get home!"

"That's the spirit!" Jessi said.

Grace raised both hands in the air. "Wave your hands both up and down. Because the Kicks don't mess around!"

The rest of us raised our hands and chanted together. "Put your hands up, wave them around. Because the Kicks don't mess around!"

Scott walked past our table and smiled. "If you girls play with that much energy, I'll definitely be at your game."

"Saturday at eleven o'clock!" Jessi called out to him, and we all laughed.

I felt a little less worried than when we had started the meeting. So far we'd convinced one person to come to our game. It was a start!

CHAPTER SIX

"The first bell's going to ring in five minutes!" Jessi yelled.

"It's okay, we got this!" I said, handing her another flyer.

Jessi and I were in a mad dash to get up as many signs for the playoff game as we could. All the Kicks had met in the front hall earlier that morning and pooled the signs we'd printed out the night before. Giselle had done an amazing job on short notice, placing black text on a white background, with the silhouette of a blue girl soccer player in the lower right corner.

The Kicks need YOU!
Come see us play the
Highland Hills Hawks
in the state finals!
Saturday, 11 a.m.
on the Kentville Middle School field

Grace had divided us into teams and assigned us each a

hallway in the school. Jessi and I were plastering the walls of the seventh-grade hallway next to the auditorium.

"How many more signs do we have?" Jessi asked.

I quickly counted the ones in my hands. "Six," I said.

"Great! We should put those all around the auditorium entrance," Jessi suggested, struggling with the masking tape roll. "If I can ever get this tape unrolled. Isn't this stuff from the 1950s or something?"

"Less talking, more tape," I urged her.

Then Steven and Cody walked up.

"You guys made signs?" Cody asked.

"Obvious much?" Jessi replied. She didn't take her eyes off the tape.

"We should've thought of that," Steven said.

"What do you mean?" I asked. "Don't you have a plan to get people to come to your game?"

Steven shrugged. "Not really."

"Our games always get a lot of fans," Cody said. "More than you guys do. So we didn't think we'd need to do anything."

Jessi spun around to face him. "How do you know you get more fans than us? Do you count them?"

"No, but . . . you can just tell," Cody said.

Jessi rolled her eyes. "Excuse us. We have to finish putting these up."

Steven and Cody strolled away, and Jessi and I worked quickly to finish. I slipped into algebra just as the bell rang, which didn't give me any time to talk to Foley. He waved and smiled at me from his desk.

After class I went to homeroom. Everybody was talking about our signs, and Frida had posted on SnapFace earlier that morning. I took out my phone to check the notification. It was a photo of the Kicks after we'd won our first playoff game, jumping up and down in a circle. Frida's mom must have taken it.

Let's Hear It for the Girls!

Semifinal Game Saturday at 11 a.m. at Kentville Middle School

#EqualPay #GirlsRule #GirlsSoccer #KentvilleSports #Kentville #YouthSoccer #SoccerPlayoffs #KentvilleMiddleSchool #KicksRule

"Do you think you used enough hashtags?" I teased her as she sat down at the desk next to me.

Frida shook her head. "No way! I should have used more. Hashtag 'Go, Kicks.' Hashtag 'Support the Girls.' Hashtag 'Girls Will Win.' I kept thinking of more right after I posted it."

Zoe joined us. "It's great, Frida," she said. "I got all of my sisters to come. And they're bringing their friends. I think we're gonna have a great turnout."

"I hope so," I said, and then I realized something. "You know, we're so worried about proving something to the boys that we haven't even talked about the game. Is anybody nervous about playing the Hawks?"

"Well, now I am," Zoe said.

"Sorry," I said, and I took a deep breath. "Tomorrow's going to be an intense day!"

• • •

When I arrived at the field the next morning to warm up before the game, I saw Foley and a bunch of other kids from our class huddled together.

"Hi, Foley!" I said, walking up to him.

"Hi, Devin!" he replied, and he held out a clipboard. "We're all set. We've got three counters for each game, so if we all get different numbers, we can average them out."

"Wow, that's impressive," I said, and I nodded to a girl next to him who was holding a small metal device in her hand. "What are those?"

"We're using tally counters," he said. "We bought them with the math club budget."

"No way!" I cried. "That's really nice of you. Of all of you."

Foley blushed. "Well, we wanted to do it right. It's kind of a fun project. Except, this morning we realized that there's a snag."

I frowned. "A snag?"

He nodded. "Well, two snags. The boys' game is right after the girls' game."

"It is?" I don't know why I hadn't known that.

"Yeah, and so it's going to be tricky to count who's leaving the girl's game and who's coming to the boy's game. And some people might get up to use the bathroom or something during the game, and then if they come back, we might count them twice," he said.

"Right," I said. "That makes sense."

"We think we've worked it out," Foley went on. "And

Mrs. Van Dyck, the math team adviser, is helping us calculate a margin of error."

I was good at math, but this was new to me. "What do you mean?"

"It means that the final number will be accurate within a certain range—plus or minus a few percentage points," he replied. "If there's a big difference between the number of fans at each game, it will be pretty easy to determine a winner. But if it's close . . ."

"I get it," I said. "Well, let's hope we win in a landslide, then. The game *and* this contest!"

Foley smiled. "I hope you do too."

"Well, I'd better go," I said, and I jogged off to join my teammates. As we stretched, the Hawks arrived in a bright-red-and-yellow bus and streamed onto the field in their matching uniforms.

"Wow, they look so . . . *clean*," Jessi remarked.

I knew what she meant. Their uniforms looked brand new, and each player wore her hair neatly pulled back. And they all had that fresh look, like they'd just woken up from a good sleep.

I looked down at my own blue Kicks jersey, which had grass stains on it that I couldn't get out. And I was wearing purple socks with yellow polka dots, because before each game we swapped one sock with one of our teammates. We kind of competed to see who could wear the craziest socks.

"I guess we look like classic underdogs," I said. "But

that doesn't matter. You can't play soccer without getting dirty!"

Then Coach called out to us to get onto the field, and we did some dribbling and passing drills. I kicked a high pass to Frida, who headed it back to me.

"Nice!" I said. "That's a new move for you, Frida."

"I am Diana, Princess of the Amazons," she replied. "Also known as Wonder Woman!"

To get over being nervous on the soccer field, Frida always pretended she was someone else. She said that getting into character helped her become a better defender.

"I'm glad you're on *my* team, then!" I said.

After our drills we sat down for the sock swap. I ended up with a green-and-white-striped sock from Grace, and combined with my purple polka-dotted sock, I looked kind of silly—but that was fine. The sock swap almost always brought us good luck!

When we had finished, Coach called us into a huddle.

"I am so proud of how far you girls have come," she said. "I know that the Hawks are fast, so we're bumping up our defense for this game. We'll have three forwards, three midfielders, and four defenders."

I looked at Grace, and we both nodded.

"Line up on the sideline," Coach instructed. "Grace, head out there for the coin toss. They're going to announce the starting players. Then we'll huddle again, and then it's game time!"

Grace jogged out onto the field with the Hawks captain.

The ref tossed the coin, and when it landed, the Hawks player pumped her fist in victory. She pointed toward the goal in front of her.

Grace jogged back and gave an apologetic shrug. I shrugged back. Not much you can do about a coin toss! Before we got into a huddle, I couldn't help noticing the huge crowd of fans on the Kicks side of the field. I had a better view when Mr. Ahmadi announced my name as a starting player, and I jogged onto the field. The stands were as packed as they'd been for a high school football game in the fall. I couldn't believe it! Foley caught my attention, grinned, and gave me a thumbs-up.

I guess I don't have to worry about the contest with the boys, I thought. *Now I just have to concentrate on the game!*

Back on the sideline for a quick huddle, we launched into one of our favorite cheers.

"I believe!" Grace and I shouted.

"I believe!" everyone repeated.

"I believe that we . . ."

"I believe that we . . ."

"I believe that we can win!"

"I believe that we can win!"

Then we repeated it together. "I believe that we can win!"

I raced off the sideline with the other Kicks starting players: Grace, Megan, Jessi, Taylor, Hailey, Frida, Jade, Anjali, Sarah, and Emma. We took our places. The Hawks had the ball, and their striker kicked it behind herself to one of their midfielders. The midfielder kicked it forward, but Grace swept in to intercept it. She passed it to me, but one of the Hawks came between us and punted it high into the air toward the Kicks goal.

One of the Hawks stopped it with her chest, and then passed it to her teammate. That player's kick went wide, and the ball zoomed right to Jessi in our midfield! Jessi dribbled down to the Hawks goal and, in her speed, sent the ball spinning out-of-bounds.

She frowned as one of the Hawks picked it up and brought it into the corner for the kick. The Hawks passed it between each other, and I tried to intercept it, with no luck.

One of the Hawks took the ball down to the Kicks goal. When our defenders swarmed her, she sent it soaring wildly over the top of the goalpost.

Sarah put the ball back in play and kicked it in to Frida, who dribbled as far as she could go and then passed it to Megan. Two Hawks surrounded Megan, so she got rid of the ball by booting it high into the air. I ran to it, stopped it with my chest, and then tore down the field. The Hawks had three defenders waiting for me, but I plowed past them and sent the ball spiraling into the goal, right past the unprepared keeper.

"That is Devin Burke of the Kicks making the first goal of this semifinal game," Mr. Ahmadi announced.

I high-fived Grace. We were off to a good start! And the momentum didn't stop, because two minutes later

Grace scored a goal after Jessi intercepted the ball and passed it to her.

And that's when the Hawks' parents started behaving *really* badly.

I hadn't been expecting it from fans of the clean-cut Hawks. But after Grace's second goal, they pounced. It happened just a few minutes later, when Megan kicked the ball high to me and it touched my arm before hitting the ground.

"Handling!" one of the parents yelled. I paused for a microsecond. But the ref hadn't blown the whistle. It wouldn't have made sense for the ref to, because I hadn't *stopped* the ball with my arm, or tried to catch the ball, which would have been handling and would have meant that the Hawks would gain possession. The ball had just happened to hit my arm. I dribbled it down the field and passed it to Jessi.

"Handling! Handling!" The parent, a blond mom, was at the fence now, screaming at the ref at the top of her lungs. The ref just looked at her and shook his head.

I didn't let it rattle me, and kept playing. At the end of the first half the Kicks were up, 3–0. Right after the second half started, Taylor made a pass and the ball skidded along the boundary line. Grace swooped in behind it and kicked it over to me. I was taking it toward the Hawks goal when I heard more yelling from the Hawks side.

"Out-of-bounds! That was out-of-bounds!"

This time it was a Hawks dad, and he marched right up

to the Hawks coach and started yelling at her. The coach had to call a time-out, and the ref went over and tried to explain to the dad that in soccer, the ball isn't out of bounds unless the entire ball crosses the line.

Coach Flores called us over during the time-out.

"The Hawks parents are getting scared that their kids are going to lose," she said. "So it looks like they're going to challenge everything. Ignore it. Pay attention to the ref only. Don't lose focus. You got this!"

"We got this!" we all repeated, and we headed back onto the field.

I made another goal a few minutes later, bringing the score to 4–0. A minute after that, somebody started yelling that Anjali had fouled another player, when she hadn't. Luckily, the ref was ignoring the parents, and so did we.

We ended the half with a score of Kicks 4, Hawks 0. I sat out the third quarter and watched the game unfold in front of me. The Hawks scored a point early on, and after that the Hawks parents started yelling at their own kids:

"Faster!"

"Get her! Get on the ball!"

"Pass it!"

We'd had a problem like this once before, with Megan's dad, but that had stopped once Coach had talked to him. The poor Hawks players were dealing with a chorus of parents, and I think it got to them. They got one more point in the third quarter, and that was it. Hailey scored in the third quarter, and Zoe and I had each made a goal in the last half. Which meant . . .

"The Kentville Kicks win, 7–2! They advance to the finals!"

We slapped hands with the Hawks and then attacked each other in a massive, screaming hug of joy.

"We did it!" Jessi shrieked.

"I BELIEVE THAT WE CAN WIN!" we shouted.

Then we had to leave the field to make way for the boys.

"I'm SO hungry!" Emma said. "Let's get hot dogs!"

"I'm in," Jessi said.

"Me too," I added.

"You guys go for it. I would rather eat field turf than a snack bar hot dog," Frida joked.

"I'll catch up with you," Zoe said. "Sabine came, and I want to say hi."

As she jogged away, Jessi raised an eyebrow. "Do you think Zoe is crushing on Sabine?"

"I've been wondering the same thing," I said. "But I feel like she would have told us by now, right?"

"Oh my gosh, they would make such a cute couple!" Emma said, clapping her hands.

Before we could discuss Zoe further, Mom, Dad, and Maisie found me.

"Great job, kiddo!" Dad cried, and he squashed me in a hug.

"All of you girls did a great job!" Mom said, looking at Jessi and Emma.

Maisie waved the sign she had made for the game that said GIRLS RULE in blue glitter marker. "I was rooting for you!"

"Do you need a ride home, honey, or are you going to stay for the boys' game?" Mom asked. "It looks like a lot of people are staying for both."

I glanced at the stands. Mom was right. They were still pretty full of people, and a lot of them were going from the stands right to the snack bar line, instead of to the gates.

"Well, that's not fair," Jessi said. "Then our fans will count as their fans."

"But if the same person is there for both games, then they *should* count as two people," Emma said.

"Foley says the way they work it out will be fair," I told them. "I trust him."

"Well, text me if you need a ride," Mom said. "And don't eat too much junk!"

I downed a hot dog, and then Jessi, Emma, and I split an order of nachos. After that we headed over to the stands. The boys' game had already started, and we found Frida by Foley and the math kids with their counters.

"We had three hundred sixty-seven people on the Kicks side during our game," Frida announced.

"That's great!" I said. "What about the boys?"

"We're going to end the count at halftime, like we did with your game," Foley said. "Like I told you, it's tricky, because a lot of people stayed. And it's hard to tell if someone is new or just coming from the snack bar. So we're going to count people in the seats and on the sidelines at halftime and compare our numbers."

After Foley said that, I paid more attention to what he and the counters were doing than to the boys' game. Before I knew it, the first half was over, and the scoreboard showed the Kangaroos with a three-point lead over the Hawks.

"It's halftime!" Jessi announced. "Foley, who won?"

"I think we should wait until everybody can hear the results, including the boys' team," Foley replied, and Jessi groaned.

"The suspense is killing me!" she complained.

"Come on, let's watch the game," I urged, pulling her to a seat with a better view.

Just like they'd done in our game, the Hawks parents yelled at the refs and their kids. But the Kangaroos played hard, and won, 7–6!

The boys whooped, they cheered, they ran around. Then Jessi corralled Cody and Steven and brought them over to Foley.

"Okay," she said. "Tell us. Who won?"

"Congratulations on making the finals," I said, before Foley could answer.

"Yeah, we both did," Steven said, smiling. "That's pretty awesome."

That smile reminded me of the old Steven—the Steven I've known since the day I met him.

Am I making too much of a big deal about this one thing? I wondered. *So what if we don't agree? We still have lots of other things in common.*

Then I looked at Foley. I had to admit that I was crushing a little bit on him, too. It was really nice that he agreed with me that women soccer players should get paid the same as men. And he was doing so much to help us settle the argument with the boys. . . .

"Come on, Foley! I need to know!" Jessi pleaded.

Foley cleared his throat. "So, the results are . . . inconclusive."

"What do you mean?" Emma asked.

"Well, our final count for the Kicks was three hundred sixty-seven, and for the boys, three hundred fifty-nine," he said.

"Woo-hoo! We won!" Jessi cheered.

"Not exactly," Foley said. "Because of the difficulties in getting an exact count, Mrs. Van Dyck says there's a margin of error of plus or minus three percent. So basically, it's a tie."

"This is ridiculous," Jessi said. "We should just call it by the numbers."

"Look at it this way, Jessi," Frida said. "If it were the other way around, you might not be arguing with Foley right now."

Jessi frowned, and I turned to Steven. "So it's a tie. Which still proves my point," I said. "Women get just as many fans as men."

"Maybe," he said slowly. "But we still have one more chance to settle this, right? We're both in the finals."

Foley nodded. "That would be an even more accurate count, because you'll be playing on different days."

"How did you know that?" I asked.

"I checked the playoff schedules online," Foley replied.

"Perfect!" Jessi said. "Let's settle this once and for all!"

"Fine with me," Cody said.

I looked at Foley. "What about you guys? You don't mind counting again?"

"It's kind of fun," he said. "Plus, we're getting extra credit."

"Okay, then," I said.

The Kicks might have won the semifinals, but it looked like we had two more battles to win!

CHAPTER SEVEN

"Cheers!" the Kicks yelled happily as we clinked our glasses together at Pizza Kitchen. We were celebrating our win from the morning and waiting for our pizzas. Even though I had scarfed down a hot dog and nachos after our game, I was still hungry. Playing soccer really worked up an appetite!

"Oops!" I said, iced tea sloshing out of my cup.

"Devin! You need a license to handle liquids!" Zoe teased. "You almost spilled iced tea on me."

Everyone was feeling lighthearted and silly. This was a big victory for us! While Coach Flores chatted with some of the players' moms at another table, we excitedly went through a play-by-play of the game.

"That was a great goal in the first half," Grace told me. "You really had defense all over you."

"That's thanks to Megan," I said modestly. "It's a miracle she got the ball through them to me."

We chatted more about game details, and then Jess mentioned how the Hawks' parents had behaved.

She shook her head. "It was very distracting. I found it really hard to focus with all of their yelling."

Hailey agreed. "I wanted to tell them all to shut up!"

Megan blushed. "I felt so bad for the Hawks. I know what that's like. It puts more pressure on you, and it's totally embarrassing."

Zoe made a sad face. "I hope they're not getting chewed out by their parents right now."

Frida raised her cup solemnly. "To the Hawks."

"To the Hawks," everyone else said, before we clinked our glasses together again, this time without all the giggling and joking.

"So," I said, ready to change the subject. "Even though we won our game and are playing for the championship, the other important competition today ended in a draw. We didn't get a ton more fans in the stands than the boys' team."

This raised some questions, and I explained everything Foley had said.

"That means next weekend will have to be what settles this once and for all," I said. "The boys play on Saturday, and we play on Sunday."

Jessi jumped in. "That means they can't steal our fans this time!"

I nodded. "That's right, but we've got to come up with a great idea to pack the stands. Any thoughts?"

"I think inviting at least ten people helped a lot," Giselle said. "Between my brothers, sisters, aunts, uncles, and cousins, I had eighteen show up."

Grace agreed. "I got some of my cousins to come today too. And since next Sunday is for the playoff championship, I think I can get even more."

I pulled a notebook out of my backpack and started taking notes. "Invite at least ten people. Got it."

"The posters around school and the social media posts definitely helped too," Jessi said. "We should do that again for sure."

"Maybe we can put flyers up around town?" Zoe suggested. "I bet Sally will let us hang one up in her store."

"And there's that coffee shop on Pacific Street," Taylor mentioned.

"The eighth graders will handle the flyers," Grace said. "We'll get them into as many shops as we can."

"Yes, cool." I made a note of it.

Frida leaned back from the table and arched an eyebrow. "These are all helpful and they absolutely need to be done, but we gotta think bigger."

Emma shrugged. "We already said we can't afford skywriting."

"No, but I've got a great plan for free advertising that could reach millions. It wouldn't cost a cent," Frida said, and then she smiled mysteriously.

"Well, out with it!" Jessi said impatiently.

"I'm surprised I didn't think of it before," Frida said,

prolonging the suspense once she knew she had everyone's attention. "It's so obvious."

Jessi gave a frustrated groan. "Not to us! Spill it."

"I am going to ask Brady McCoy to come to our game," she announced triumphantly. "Remember when he came to our fund-raiser for the elementary school soccer team?"

Emma's eyes were wide and shining at the mention of her idol. "How could I ever forget? It was the happiest moment of my life!"

"Do you think he would come again?" Grace asked.

"He's really busy, so I'm not sure," Frida said. "I know equality is very important to him. And he's a huge soccer fan. I know he retweeted a lot of the #EqualPay posts by Abby Wambach and other US women's team members, so he'll totally support our cause. But he might still be on tour. If he's available, I know he'll try to make it. And everyone will want to come to the game if they think a celebrity will be there!"

We all got quiet for a second. Having Brady McCoy would be a huge advantage for us!

Zoe broke the silence. "Do you think that's too much of a gimmick? Shouldn't we be able to attract fans based on our soccer skills and not because of a celebrity?"

That made me think. "I see your point, Zoe," I said thoughtfully. "But we need to get a lot of people to listen to us about this. Women athletes should be treated the same as men. Brady can get us a bigger audience and more people to hear our message. We might even change people's opinions or make them aware if they didn't know this was happening. I say we do it."

Heads were nodding in agreement. I looked at Zoe. She smiled.

"Let's shout it from the rooftops, then!" she said, her voice mirroring her enthusiasm.

"When are you going to ask him?" Hailey asked.

Frida whipped out her phone. "I'll text him right now."

Emma's eyes got so big, I thought they might pop right out of her head. "You have his phone number?"

Frida smiled again. "I do."

Emma lunged for Frida's phone, but Frida held it over her head. "I had to promise not to give it out to anyone. He has to change the number all the time because it gets leaked."

Emma sighed and slumped back in her chair. "Fine."

"We should have a backup plan in case he can't be there," I said as Frida texted Brady.

"I'm going to ask him to share it on social media too, and invite his fans and famous friends to attend," Frida said. "If he does, that will get us tons of publicity and more people to support the cause of equal pay."

"Wow, we could go viral!" Megan said.

"But what if he doesn't share it? We need to have a plan B," I insisted.

"I'm also going to ask Miriam to share it on her social and invite all her friends to come," Frida announced.

"Isn't Miriam in her nineties?" Jessi asked. Miriam was

an elderly woman Frida had met while the Kicks had been volunteering in a nursing home. "Does she even know what social media is?"

Frida scoffed, waving her hand like she was swatting away Jessi's words. "Yes, of course. She's got a few hundred thousand followers on Twitter."

"Oh wow," I said. "If we can get her and Brady to post about it once or twice, that should help our cause."

"Miriam has some famous friends," Frida shared. "She was an inspiration to a lot of actors, and she says some famous movie stars still visit her to ask for advice. If she says this issue is important, they'll listen to her. Maybe *she* can get a celebrity to come show support."

I was furiously writing all the details down in my notebook. I read back everything we had discussed. "So our plan is for each of us to personally invite ten people, post on social using the hashtags again, and put posters up around school and Kentville. And Frida will reach out to Brady McCoy and Miriam to see if they will come, invite their famous friends, and share on social. What does everyone think?"

"I think we should ask our parents to take flyers to work and see if they can hang them up there, too," Taylor suggested.

I added that to my list. "Anything else?"

Everyone looked around the table at one another before Grace answered.

"I think we've got our plan!" she said, smiling.

"Okay, we'll check in with one another throughout the week before practice," I told the group. "The only day we don't have practice is Tuesday, but we can always text if something urgent comes up."

"Oh man!" Jessi gleefully rubbed her hands together. "The boys won't know what hit them. I hope they come to our game, so we can see their faces when we've got so many fans, there isn't enough room for everyone!"

With that, the pizzas were delivered to the table, and we all dug in.

The waiter put a pizza topped with white, gold, and purple cauliflower; shaved Parmesan; and garlic in front of me and Zoe. We were the only ones who wanted the garlicky cauliflower pie.

Jessi wrinkled her nose. "Ugh, Devin, why would you ruin perfectly good pizza by putting cauliflower on it?" she asked as she grabbed a piece of pepperoni from her own pizza.

"I like what I like." I shrugged. "It's delicious. You should try it."

Jessi stuck out her tongue. "Yuck, no thanks. I'll stick to my pepperoni."

"You don't know what you're missing, Jessi," Zoe said as she nibbled on the end of her cauliflower slice, before she put it down suddenly on her plate. "I just remembered! I posted Emma's session on *Fashion from A to Zoe* this morning before the game. With all the excitement, I forgot to show it to anyone, even Emma."

Emma squealed as she pulled up Zoe's blog on her phone. We all followed suit, looking for Zoe's latest post.

"Oh no. I don't know if I can see it. I'm sure I look like a total dork." Emma squeezed her eyes shut tight.

My eyes widened in surprise as a photo of Emma filled the screen, in a white, flowy top with lace trim around the bottom and around the three-quarter-length sleeves. It topped off her denim shorts and pink tennis shoes. Zoe had styled her with rose-gold mirrored sunglasses and a pink-and-white bandanna tying back her long, black hair.

"Emma! This photo is incredible. Beautiful, but laid back and fun. It's so you!" I exclaimed.

Emma opened her right eye a little bit. "Is it safe to look?"

"It's more than safe!" Jessi said. "You're so pretty in these pictures!"

Emma opened her eyes all the way and stared at her phone screen. She gave a little gasp of surprise. "I do look kind of cute!"

Frida shook her head. "Oh, Emma, hiding in your shell doesn't help you, or the world. Let your light shine!" she said, like she was reciting a line in a movie.

Though Frida was over-the-top as always, she had a point.

"Emma, you are so natural in your own skin that it makes everyone comfortable around you," Zoe said. "That's a gift."

In another photo, Emma wore white capri pants with navy-blue stripes running down the length of her legs.

Zoe had rolled up the cuffs and finished the outfit with a matching navy T-shirt and a long silver necklace with a heart dangling from it. Emma's hair fell in soft waves around her face, and Yvette had added a little gloss to her lips and some highlighter on her brow bone. She looked casual yet put together.

"My mom bought me those pants months ago," Emma said. "I didn't know what to wear them with, but when Zoe was digging through my closet, she knew just what to do."

Zoe had titled the blog post "Looks for a Casual Cutie," and her tips were to always choose comfortable clothes. *If you feel good wearing it, you'll look good.* She also suggested styling comfortable jogging pants or jeans with silk tees and stylish sneakers or a printed blouse and flats.

"You look fun and friendly in all of those photos," Jessi remarked. "That's so *you*, Emma!"

"I'll take 'fun' or 'friendly' over 'weird and dorky' any day," Emma joked.

"Oh, this one is so cute!" Frida cried, pointing to a photo of Emma in high-waisted dark blue polka-dotted shorts and a floral silk tee with LONDON scrawled across it. She sat on a swing, and Zoe had taken the photo midlaugh.

"We went to the park near my house for this one," Zoe said.

"What about dresses?" Grace asked. The rest of the Kicks had their phones out and were scrolling through Zoe's blog. "Did you model any dresses, Emma?"

"I sort of hate dresses, but Zoe found a nice one for me," Emma answered. "It's the fifth or sixth photo, I think."

We all scrolled until we found it: Emma in a green, flowy high-neck dress with pleats and a ruffled sleeve that hit right around her elbow. The dress fell to just above her knee, and she wore a pair of simple tan sandals and a floral headband.

"Oh wow, that's fabulous!" Megan cried.

"Zoe's sister Opal lent it to me. It was so comfortable!" Emma said. "I might have to ask my mom to get one for me."

The photos were beautiful, and I was so glad Emma liked them and was happy with how they'd turned out.

"You're up next, Devin!" Zoe said. "When can you do it?"

Seeing how awesome Frida's and Emma's shoots had turned out made me excited. Yes, I'd done some modeling before, but this would be all about me and *my* personality, not trying to sell something to someone else. I couldn't wait.

"How about Tuesday after school, since we don't have practice?" I asked.

"I'll put it in my calendar," Zoe said, and we all dug back into our pizza.

Not only would the photo shoot be fun, but it would give me a chance to leave the drama of the Kangaroos versus Kicks behind me for a moment!

CHAPTER EIGHT

"I'm ready for my close-up!" I tried to do my best Frida impersonation when Zoe opened the door to her house Tuesday after school. Zoe burst out laughing as she grabbed my arm and pulled me through the door. I guess I couldn't pull off dramatic like Frida does.

"Did you bring everything I told you to?" Zoe asked as she grabbed the duffel bag I had packed the night before, based on her explicit instructions.

"Yes, Sergeant Fashion!" I said, giving her a mock salute.

"We'll see about that," Zoe said as she led the way to her room. She dropped my bag onto her bed, unzipped it, and started going through it, tossing clothes onto the bed.

While she was doing that, I was amazed to see that one corner of her room had been completely redone. Where there used to be a comfy, plush chair and an ottoman, there was now a mini-photo studio. A white backdrop hung against the wall, with a tall stool placed in the center. Professional lights, like the ones I had seen when I had done those modeling shoots, were on stands facing the backdrop. A fancy, expensive-looking camera was attached to a tripod.

I gasped and turned to Zoe. "No wonder your photos look so amazing. You've got a totally professional setup here. I didn't know you were that serious about your blog. I'm impressed."

"I'm really lucky that I was able to use some of my bat mitzvah money to buy the camera and the lights," she explained. "At first I didn't think my mom and dad were going to let me, but Mom finally said yes, as long as I put the rest in my college fund and promised not to use it for anything else. I'm so happy about the setup." She beamed as she looked at it.

"But now," she said, turning her full attention back to me, "it's time to focus on you and what your first look is going to be."

She went back to pawing through the items in my duffel bag. "Hmmm . . ." She was very thoughtful before she pulled out a pair of jogging pants and a black sweatshirt. "Let's try this first, but before we get you changed, let me get Yvette."

Zoe left the room and returned with her sister. Yvette looked a lot like Zoe, with the same strawberry-blond hair, but hers was much longer and pulled back into a messy bun on top of her head. She was wearing sweats that had old paint splatters on them and a T-shirt.

"I told you I had to work on my art project today," Yvette was protesting as Zoe led her into the room, but when she saw me, her eyes lit up. "Oh, look at those cheekbones. A little contouring, and they'll pop!" she said excitedly.

Zoe pulled the stool over to her bed, and I perched on it while Yvette went to work, with lotions and creams that smelled great, and tiny little brushes that tickled my skin. I started to relax, and she chattered as she worked.

"I can't decide if I want to do fine art or go into cosmetology. I love them both," Yvette said. "Mom says to get the cosmetology degree while I'm getting a college degree in art, and that way I'll always have a way to make steady income. So I might end up doing both!"

I didn't know Yvette very well because even though she and Zoe were sisters, they were very different. Yvette was extroverted and hung out with the art and drama kids. Zoe was more of an introvert, and she spent most of her time playing soccer.

"In elementary school, people thought we were twins," Zoe had told me once. "I hated that. I wanted my own identity!"

Yvette stopped brushing my face, stepped back, and squinted at me. Then she nodded, pleased.

"That's a natural makeup look that should go with everything," she explained. Then she turned to Zoe. "If you have something more glam you're dressing her in, I'd try this red lipstick. It'll give her lips a pop and add some drama."

"What about my hair?" I asked as my hand crept up to my messy ponytail.

"Don't worry," Zoe said confidently. "I've got my curling iron and straightener plugged in. I can change up your looks as we go."

For my first outfit, Zoe had me wear a pair of my own dark beige joggers—loose-fitting pants that were banded at the ankles—with a black sweatshirt that my mom had bought me when we'd first moved to Cali that said CALIFORNIA GIRL on it. Zoe frowned over my choice of sneakers. Then she ran into her sister Opal's room and came back with a pair of white Converse high-tops. Out of her own closet she pulled an infinity scarf to top off the look, and then handed me a chunky beige leather bag.

"I don't even use a pocketbook," I protested.

"I know, but this is all about elevating an athletic look," she explained. "You don't have to do it if you don't want to."

I remembered Emma's photo shoot, and how awesome she'd looked in that dress, even though she almost never wore them, and I nodded. "I'll do it."

"Great!" Zoe replied, and she stepped back and smiled at her finished design before piling my hair into a loose, messy bun on top of my head.

"It's perfect!" she declared. I stood in front of the white backdrop while she took the first few photos, and then she had me sit on the stool for some more. I turned, tilted, and smiled just as she directed, and we chatted throughout. It was fun and a lot less pressure than the professional shoots.

For my second look she handed me a pair of leopard-print pants in tones of pink, purple, and orange, with a black-and-white racing stripe up the side of each leg. I raised my eyebrows.

"Uh, are you sure these aren't for Jessi?" I asked.

"They're Opal's," Zoe said. "Don't worry, this is going to be killer."

Wearing the pants was way different from carrying the bag, but since I'd decided to put my trust in Zoe, I figured I might as well go all in.

"Fine," I said, and I started pulling on the pants, which was tough to do until Zoe pointed out that they had zipper ankles, and I had to unzip them before they could go over my feet. I got them on and then paired them with a swingy black cami that Zoe had asked me to bring.

"Now the shoes," Zoe said as she reached into her closet for a pair of black strappy high heels.

"But I hate walking in heels!" I complained.

"The Devin I know is not going to let a pair of shoes get the best of her," Zoe said, and I couldn't argue because she was right. She took my hair out of the bun and made some loose curls with the curling iron before slapping an oversize watch onto my wrist and a pair of sunglasses onto my face. When I looked in the mirror, I loved the finished look, even the pants. It all worked together, just as Zoe had promised.

She started shooting against the white background.

"This is good, but let's go outside," she said, and soon she was snapping photos of me as I walked down the street. At one point I saw her neighbors pull up in the driveway, and I started to feel self-conscious, but Zoe just looked at them and said, "Hello, Mr. and Mrs. Kazmi," cheerfully before zeroing in on me again.

I had to admit, it was a little hard walking in those high heels on the sidewalk. I'd never worn heels that high before, but as least I didn't fall on my face.

The third outfit started with a denim jacket that I had borrowed from my mom when Zoe'd asked if I had one.

"And so it begins," my mom had said with a rueful smile when she'd given it to me.

"What do you mean?" I wondered.

"My sister and I always used to borrow each other's stuff, and my mom's, too, especially her shoes, since we were all the same size." She shook her head at the memory. "That caused a couple of fights, I can tell you."

I didn't really think I'd ever borrow my mom's clothes a lot, but the jacket was cute, and Zoe had me wear it with a white V-neck T-shirt, which she tucked into one of her sister Jayne's knee-length gray pencil skirts. I wore my own pair of Kicks blue sneakers.

"Fabulous!" Zoe said, and she took photos of me both inside and outside, sitting on her family's porch swing and walking through the backyard.

"Whew!" I said as I changed out of the latest outfit. "I'm actually getting tired. Are we almost done?"

A huge smile broke out over Zoe's face. "I saved the best for last, and I'm so excited. I made something special for you," she said as she disappeared into her closet again.

Zoe came out holding a white scoop-neck T-shirt. In black letters emblazoned across the front was #EQUALPAY.

I jumped as I squealed. "I love it. This is perfect! Thank you, Zoe. How did you do this?"

"They're just iron-on letters from the craft store," Zoe said with a shrug, but she looked proud.

"What a great idea!" I was all smiles. Talk about being able to express my personality. This was definitely all me.

"Wait till you see how I style it," she said.

Soon she had me in the T-shirt, wearing my own denim shorts with a braided black belt, topped with her sister Yvette's black leather moto jacket, and leopard pull-on sneakers borrowed from Jayne. Zoe broke out the curling iron again to make my hair extra wavy, and she arranged it spilling over my shoulders. She found yet another oversize watch and paired it with a wrist cuff on the opposite arm. It was all topped off with mirrored aviator sunglasses. I couldn't believe how glamorous I looked.

We took some shots indoors and outdoors, and with and without the sunglasses. My favorites were when Zoe broke out the soccer ball on her lawn and I got to pose with that.

At last we were done and I changed back into my own clothes. My jeans and T-shirt had never felt so comfy. We sat on Zoe's bed and looked at the photos together.

"These are amazing, Devin!" Zoe exclaimed. "You are sporty chic, and that will be the theme of your fashion profile on my blog."

"Thanks for everything," I said as I reached over and gave her a hug. "I felt like a movie star or something. I wish you could dress me every day!"

"If only I could dress the entire world. That's my goal one day," Zoe shared. "I really want to be a fashion designer."

"Going by your blog, I think you can definitely make it happen. You've got such an eye when it comes to fashion," I told her.

"What about you, Devin? Still planning on being the next soccer star?"

"Definitely." I nodded. "My dream is a soccer scholarship, and I'm going to work really hard to get it."

"When you are a famous soccer player, I'll design all your formal-wear looks," she said.

"And I'll make sure you always have the best seats at my games," I told her.

"You'd better!" Zoe said.

Then I remembered that there was something I wanted to ask her.

"So. . . ," I began. "Is Sabine going to do a shoot with you?"

Zoe's cheeks turned pink. "Yeah, she's coming over next week. We're going to take the photos, and then Sabine said we should go to the new sushi place that opened up by the beach."

"Like a date?" I asked.

Zoe sighed. "I wish! I really like Sabine, but I can't tell if she likes me back or not. How did you know that Steven had a crush on you?"

I tried to remember. "I'm not sure . . . maybe when he asked me to that school dance? And to hang out at the mall? So, if Sabine asked you to go to the sushi restaurant . . ."

Zoe's face brightened. "Maybe she *does* like me back. I hope she does."

"Emma says you would make a cute couple," I told her.

Zoe laughed. "I agree," she said. "And speaking of cute couples, what's with you and Foley?"

Now I could feel *my* cheeks turn pink. "What do you mean?" I asked.

"You know what I mean," Zoe said. "Whenever you're around him, you can't take your eyes off him."

"He's so nice!" I blurted out. "He's being a lot nicer than Steven about this whole equal pay thing."

At that moment Zoe's phone buzzed and she picked it up to check. Her eyes got big, and she gasped.

"Devin, you are not going to believe this. Brady McCoy just tweeted about the Kicks game this Sunday. He said he's sad he can't make it, but he asked all his fans to go to support his friend Frida and equal pay!"

"What?!" I jumped off the bed, Zoe following me, and

we hugged and screamed and ran around her room.

"Do you know what this means?" Zoe asked with a smile.

"The boys don't stand a chance!" I replied.

With all of Brady McCoy's fans in our corner, I hoped Steven would understand how important this issue was to not only me but to millions of people all over the world.

CHAPTER NINE

The next morning I woke up extra early to get in some more conditioning time. While it had been nice living it up as a fashion model with Zoe the day before, I had to get down to business leading the Kicks to a championship!

The sun was just starting to rise as I pulled on jogging shorts and a T-shirt. I had to wear this dorky pullover hoodie with reflective panels on it because Mom said if I didn't wear it, I couldn't go out jogging so early in the morning. She was afraid I'd get hit by a car, but the panels bounced back light, so if a car approached, it would see me.

That wasn't her only rule. I could jog only within a two-block radius of our house, which meant I basically ran in circles. But it was the only way I could get outside to run. I wanted to be in tip-top shape for the championship!

And the final rule: no headphones. "You have to be

alert and aware of your surroundings at all times," my mom said.

That rule didn't bother me so much. Even though I didn't have my favorite songs playing, it was kind of cool to be out and awake before everybody else was up. It was peaceful and quiet, with only the sounds of the birds waking up and starting their day. It gave me time to think, and my main focus was on today's practice. We needed to run drills that would penetrate the defense of the Douglas Dragons.

Because this was the final championship game, we were playing a team we'd never faced before. Over the weekend Coach had sent Grace and me an email with what she'd heard about the Dragons. They communicated well as a team, and they were great at putting up a wall of defenders against any offense. Coach had watched some of their games she'd found online, and she said that their strategy was to aggressively cover offensive players so they couldn't get shots in when they were close to the goal.

I had some ideas about what we could do to strengthen our offense against the Dragons, with a focus on the best way to break through to get into shooting range. As I pounded the pavement around my neighborhood, I visualized the Kicks clashing with the Dragons on the soccer field, imagining many different scenarios. I wanted our team to be prepared for them all!

That's the determination I arrived with at the soccer field after school on Wednesday for practice. I had been so focused on the finals and how we as a team could beat the Dragons that I hadn't spent much time thinking about the whole boys-versus-girls thing. But as soon as I arrived at the field, I could tell this was not going to be any ordinary practice!

There were several TV news vans, and reporters with microphones and camera crews on the sidelines. I jogged over quickly, curious to see what was going on, and saw that Coach Flores and Principal Gallegos were each being interviewed by separate reporters.

Jessi, Emma, Zoe, and Frida ran up to me. Jessi grabbed my arm.

"Isn't this wild?" she asked.

I looked around at the scene, and my jaw dropped. "What's going on? Are they here because we made the finals?"

Frida smiled and held up her phone. "They're all here because of Brady McCoy. His tweet went viral, and everyone is talking about the Kicks!"

I grabbed Frida's phone and started scrolling. His tweet had hundreds of thousands of likes and many replies like *We love you, Brady! We'll be there! Real McCoys are real Kicks fans, too!* ("Real McCoys" was what the members of Brady's fan club called themselves. Emma was one!)

"It's unbelievable, right?" Emma said. "We're, like, totally in the public eye now."

The other Kicks came over. Grace shook her head. "I can't believe how this has blown up."

I sighed. "Sure, it's great, but how are we going to practice with a media circus going on?"

Grace looked me in the eyes and nodded. She was as competitive as I was, and I knew she wanted to win the finals just as much.

Coach Flores walked over with Principal Gallegos next to her and blew her whistle, getting all the Kicks to come huddle around her.

"As I'm sure you've noticed, we've got some members of the media here who want to watch us practice," she said. "They've also requested to speak with some of you."

Principal Gallegos jumped in. "We made it perfectly clear to them that none of you can be interviewed on camera without parental permission. So please do not speak with any of the reporters."

"They will be taking some video during practice," Coach Flores explained. "I checked, and I've got signed permission slips from all of your parents to have your photos taken at school events, so we've allowed the camera crews to stay and film."

Brianna's hand shot up. "What are they doing here?"

"As some of you know," Coach started, with a look at Frida, who gave her a proud smile, "the pop star Brady McCoy has been on social media talking about our final match this Sunday. His comments have generated a lot of interest, especially about the subject of equal pay in professional soccer, and about the wager between the Kentville boys' and girls' teams."

At this, Grace and I exchanged guilty glances. It hadn't even occurred to me to tell Coach about our bet with the boys.

Coach continued. "I admire the spirit behind the wager, and I understand how the perception of being treated unfairly can be very frustrating. I know firsthand what a talented, hardworking team of soccer players I coach. Each and every one of you puts a hundred percent into practices and games, and I am so proud of my team."

Megan let out a "Whoop!" and some of the girls clapped.

"But I want to make one thing clear," Coach went on. "The best way for you to prove you are as good as the boys' team and shouldn't be treated differently is on the field. Play your best. Emma and Zarine, continue to make your amazing saves in the goal. And our awesome defense players like Giselle and Frida, keep making it hard for our opponents to find the back of that net. Alandra and all our other midfielders, maintain that great communication and stamina that keeps the ball pushing forward. And our strikers, and our co-captains, Grace and Devin, keep looking for those scoring opportunities. Because you know how to find them."

Grace and I high-fived.

Coach looked around at all of us and smiled. "I'm surrounded by talented players. All you have to do is show that to the world to prove your point."

Some of the girls cheered, and I knew Coach was right. But I couldn't help thinking that the women's team had won the World Cup, and they'd still gotten paid less than the men. And if winning the World Cup wasn't proving a point, then what would?

Principal Gallegos stepped forward and tugged nervously on his tie before he began to speak.

"Coach Flores is correct. The best way to settle this is to prove yourselves on the field," he said. "However, the school and even the local police department are now worried about crowd control at Sunday's game, since this pop star has encouraged his fans to attend. In the future, please discuss any advertising or publicity plans with your coach or myself."

I cringed when he said that. I'd never thought of the implications of having hundreds, or maybe even thousands, of Brady McCoy fans and equal pay enthusiasts descending on our soccer field. Would we get in trouble?

"I understand these are unusual circumstances," Principal Gallegos continued. "I'd just like you all to remember this, going forward. We will have to request a police presence to help with crowd control, and that costs the town of Kentville money."

A murmur went up among us, and I knew everyone else was thinking the same thing.

"Thank you, girls," he finished. "Best of luck at the game this Sunday, but please, no more celebrity tweets!" With that, he left the field, passing the crowd of reporters, who chased after him with their microphones. It was an unusual sight, and I almost felt like pinching my arm to see if I was dreaming.

"Coach?" Grace said, raising her hand.

"Yes, Grace?" Coach smiled at her. One of the things I liked best about Coach Flores was how nice she always was. When I'd first joined the Kicks, I'd had to ask her on behalf of the team to be a little tougher. Not mean, but stricter when it came to practice, and to push us a little bit. She took that feedback, and now she was the perfect coach, kind yet able to get the best out of her players.

"As co-captain, I want to say on behalf of the team, we never meant to cause any problems," Grace said.

"I understand." Coach smiled kindly again. "Who could ever imagine a scenario like this? Yet I must say, I admire your ability to get things done and to take on a challenge. Those skills will serve you well, not only on the soccer field but in life."

I raised my hand. "I want to say that we've given everything to make it to the championship, and I don't want any of us to get distracted now with all the cameras and Brady McCoy stuff. Let's just keep our focus the way we have the entire season. I know it will be tougher with everything going on, but we can do it. Let's put our all into this practice. The Kicks will be league champs!"

Everyone cheered again, and we got into a circle and threw our arms around one another. Then Jessi started us chanting a familiar soccer cheer: "Kick that ball and make a score. Come on, team, we wanna see more! Move those feet 'cause victory is sweet! Do our best, and we can't be beat!"

We jumped around as we chanted, and when we broke the huddle, we saw a camera aimed at us from across the field.

"If they thought that was good, let's show 'em how it's really done!" I told my team. "Let's do it, Kicks!"

We hit the ground running, performing drills and scrimmages to have us in tip-top shape for the championship game against the Dragons. It was time to prove ourselves on the field!

Chapter Ten

At dinner that night I told my family about the TV cameras at practice.

"Wow, Devin," Dad said. "That's huge."

"I asked everyone in my class to go, and my entire soccer team," Maisie said. "Isn't that huge too?"

I smiled at her. "Yes, Maisie. Thank you!"

"You girls certainly have worked hard to get the word out," Mom remarked.

I nodded. "Yes, but Coach reminded us today that now we need to prove ourselves on the field. We're going to have to give it all we've got on Sunday."

"You always do, Devin," Dad said.

Mom looked at the clock. "It's almost time for the evening news. Let's turn it on so we don't miss the report."

Maisie ran into the living room to turn on the TV,

and by the time we'd cleaned the dinner dishes, the local sports report was coming on.

"Look! There's your coach!" Maisie squealed as Coach Flores talked to the reporter. Then the shot changed to us scrimmaging on the field. There I was, kicking the ball to Jessi! Mom, Dad, and Maisie all cheered.

The story ended with a quote from Principal Gallegos, and then the Kicks cheer.

"Who knows if that tweet from teen heartthrob Brady McCoy will fill the stands at this week's girls championship game, but the Kentville Kangaroos—affectionately known to their fans as 'the Kicks'—are hoping it will," the sportscaster finished.

The blond news anchor smiled. "Well, I know my girls are going to beg me to go to that game," she said. "They love Brady."

Then my phone started blowing up with texts.

Emma: Did u see it? That was awesome!

Frida: We look great on camera!

Jessi: We are going to destroy those boys!

Jessi's text made me pause a little bit. I never wanted to *destroy* anybody. I was just trying to prove a point.

Do the boys want to destroy us, too? I wondered.

The next morning Jessi ran up to me in the hall.

"Did you see Cody's posts?" she asked me.

"What posts?" I asked.

She thrust out her phone in front of me. Cody had

made a whole bunch of posts on social media about the Brady McCoy thing.

I guess the girls have to cheat to win this contest! with a photo of Brady McCoy's tweet.

Then he'd posted that embarrassing photo of Emma when she'd gotten hit on the head with her own shoe, defending a goal. It had happened earlier in the season, and it had devastated Emma. But we'd thought the episode was over.

The Kangaroos don't need celebrities to get people to come to our games, he'd written. *We've got talent.*

Jessi's eyes were flashing with anger. "What the heck?" she asked. "How dare he bring up Emma again? And who said using Brady McCoy was cheating? We never made any rules!"

"This is pretty bad," I agreed, and I scrolled through the post's likes. Most of the names were players on the boys' soccer team—including Steven. I felt a lump in my stomach.

Jessi took the phone back from me. "I'm going to reply," she said, and she started typing. I put my hand on top of hers.

"Don't!" I said. "There's no way to win a fight on social media, Jessi. You know that. Let's talk to them later, in person."

Jessi frowned but put her phone away. "You're always so sensible, Devin," she said, and then she rolled her head in a circle. "I'll try to wait until lunchtime. But if I explode before then, you'll know why."

Fortunately, for the rest of the morning, most people were congratulating us about the news report.

Foley stopped me in the hallway. "I guess you know the Kicks were on TV last night," he said. "Everybody's talking about it."

"Yeah, I saw some of it," I said. "I think we're really going to pack the place!"

He smiled. "You've made our job a lot harder," he said, and then he moved his pointer finger up and down, like he was pressing a button. "We're going to be really busy!"

I laughed. "Thanks again for doing this. It's really nice of you."

Foley blushed, and there was an awkward silence for a second.

"So, see you," I said.

"Yeah, later," he replied, still blushing, and I headed to my class.

Jessi kept her cool with Cody and Steven all morning, even during gym class. But at lunchtime she slammed her stuff down onto our table and marched over to the boys. I followed her.

"All right, Cody, what's your problem?" she asked, folding her arms and striking a defiant pose.

"What do you mean?" Cody asked.

"That post about us cheating," she said. "And saying we have no talent. And posting that photo of Emma. That wasn't nice."

Cody shrugged. "I was just trying to be funny, okay?" he said. "Besides, you guys *are* cheating."

"How can we be cheating, when there were no rules?" I asked him. "That doesn't make any sense."

Steven spoke up. "Maybe it's not technically cheating, but it's not fair. Just because you guys know someone famous means you have an advantage that we don't. It has nothing to do with who plays a better game of soccer."

"The point isn't who plays better," I shot back. "If that were the case, the women's pro team would be paid ten times as much as the guys, not the other way around. It's all about who can get people to come to the game. That's what you said."

"Maybe you guys are just jealous because you're not thinking creatively," Jessi said. "You didn't even put flyers up to get people to your semifinals game."

The boys didn't have an answer for that.

"Could you just please take down that picture of Emma?" I asked. "It doesn't really bother her to see it anymore, but it wasn't nice of you to do that."

Cody looked at Steven, who gave him a small nod.

"Okay, I'll take that one down," he said.

"Thanks," I said. "You know, I really hope you guys win your championship. Just because we're in this competition doesn't mean I don't want you to succeed."

"I hope you guys win too," Steven said, and he sounded like he meant it.

Jessi looked like she wanted to say more, but she followed me away from the boys' table, and we sat down with Frida, Emma, and Zoe.

"What was *that* all about?" Emma asked.

"It's about Cody's nasty posts this morning," Jessi said. "He's going to take down the photo of you."

Emma shrugged. "You guys know it doesn't bother me anymore."

"Yeah, but it's the principle of the thing," Jessi said.

"I agree," I said. "Cody is supposed to be our friend. And Steven liked the post."

"I don't know about those two," Jessi said. "I feel like maybe they're not our friends anymore."

I felt that way too, but the idea hurt so much that I didn't know what to say. Then Zoe changed the subject.

"Who wants to see Devin's photo shoot?" she asked. "It's up on the blog."

We got out our phones and checked the photos. I still couldn't believe what an amazing job Zoe had done.

"Who is that girl?" I wondered. "Is it really me?"

"Devin, stop it. You are gorgeous," Zoe said. "But thanks."

My friends all loved the sporty chic outfits.

"I hope I get to wear some leopard print too," Jessi said.

"The one of you in the skirt is my favorite," Frida said. "You should wear skirts more often."

I frowned. "Only if I had Zoe to style me every day."

"That pencil skirt is so cute," Emma said. "Zoe, you

really are giving me good ideas about how to dress up. I'm sure your blog is going to take off."

"She's already got four hundred blog subscribers," Frida said. "And that photo on Instagram of Devin in the EQUAL PAY shirt is getting tons of comments."

I clicked on that photo. Frida was right—more than fifty people had commented already!

"Look, there's a nice comment from Foley," Emma noticed. "Isn't he the math club guy?"

I scrolled and found Foley's comment.

Great T-shirt!

I smiled, and I asked myself again: *Am I starting to like Foley? Am I starting to* not *like Steven?* I know people say it's good to explore your feelings, and not bury them deep inside, but I decided to bury them deep, deep down for the moment.

Feelings were going to have to wait until after the championship game!

CHAPTER ELEVEN

"I don't think this is a good idea, Devin," Jessi said as I pulled her by the arm toward the soccer field on Saturday. The boys were in pursuit of their championship bid, and I wanted to be there to see if they won. Okay, I admit it. I also wanted to be there to see how many fans they'd gotten to show up.

"Jessi's right, Devin," Zoe complained. "If we show up to watch the boys, we'll be counted as fans for them."

Frida shook her head. "I can't stay away. I've got to see what the boys are up to, especially after all of their posts on social yesterday."

"I'm curious too," Emma replied. "'A fun surprise is planned for all fans of the Kangaroos who attend,'" Emma quoted from Cody's social media feed. "But Zoe and Jessi have a point. I don't want to give them any extra numbers. We've got to beat them!"

We were all walking to the field from the parking lot, where my mom had dropped us off. Well, some of us were walking. I was dragging Jessi!

"Come on," I insisted. "We've got to see what they have planned. And how they play. We don't have to sit in the stands."

That got Jessi's attention. "Can we sit on the Raiders side, then?"

The boys were competing against the Clarksville Raiders. "We're not actually rooting for the Raiders," I replied.

"Are you sure about that?" Jessi arched an eyebrow. "After the way Cody and Steven have been acting, I'm ready to pour out some serious Raider pride."

"Go, Raiders!" Frida gave a cheer. "Hmmm . . . I think I like the sound of that."

I stopped in my tracks and turned to face them. "We are all Kangaroos. It wouldn't be good sportsmanship to root against the boys, no matter what has happened. You wouldn't want them rooting against us tomorrow, would you?"

Emma gasped. "No! That would be so RUDE!"

I nodded. "Exactly. If we weren't in this contest with the boys, we'd all be at this game cheering them on."

Jessi crossed her arms. "But we *are* in this contest. Don't you want to win?"

"I want to win the championship even more," I said. "Come on, Jessi, we're here. If you want to sit on the Raiders side, fine. But I'm not going to be a traitor to Kentville."

Jessi frowned and scanned the field. There was a walkway from the home stands to the away stands, and it passed behind the goal. A few people were standing along the fence there to watch the game. "Let's go there," she said. "In the middle."

Zoe nodded. "That sounds like a good compromise to me. The math kids won't count us unless we watch the game from the home side."

"I think we *should* be counted. We're here to see them, not the Raiders," Emma chimed in. "But I'll do what everyone wants."

I shrugged. "Fine. Let's watch from the middle. But you can't stop me from cheering for the boys if I want to, Jessi!"

Jessi stuck her tongue out at me, and we made our way to the field. Once we got closer, we could see that the stands were full of fans, pretty much as many who'd come to our game the previous week.

Emma gulped. "You know, I was thinking that all of Brady's fans who said they were coming might have been caught up in the moment. What if they don't show? They don't really care about us, and it's not like Brady is going to be here."

Frida waved a hand around Emma's head. "Clear out that negative energy. They'll come, I know it!"

The boys were warming up. I saw Steven and Cody running some drills. Cody looked over and smiled and waved at us, and Jessi turned her back to him. Cody shook his head and kept drilling.

Then Foley walked up to us.

"Hey, shouldn't you be counting?" I asked.

"The whole math team is here today to help," he said. He held up his clicker. "Should I count you for the Kangaroos?"

"Absolutely not!" Jessi replied.

Foley raised an eyebrow and looked at me.

"Um, we're trying to stay neutral today," I explained. "We thought this was a team-free zone."

He nodded. "Yeah, we aren't counting anyone who is sitting in the Raiders section."

"That's what I said," Zoe piped up.

"You guys are really taking this seriously, aren't you?" he asked.

"Maybe too seriously," I admitted, and Foley grinned.

"I'd better get back to counting," he said. "See ya!"

Foley walked away, and Emma looked at me and wiggled her eyebrows.

"What?" I protested, but Emma only smiled in response.

Jessi looked around and scanned the bleachers. "I wonder what the big surprise is that they were talking about."

Zoe read off her phone. "Latest update is that whatever it is, it's going to take place at halftime."

Emma looked up at the sky. "Maybe they were able to hire a skywriter."

Right then the game started, and we barely spoke as we watched it unfold. I had this weird feeling of wanting the boys to win but also wanting to prove that we were just as good as, if not better than, they were. Why couldn't we all be treated the same? It frustrated me to think about it.

And frustrated was how it looked for both the Kangaroos and the Raiders. The Raiders would get the ball into the Kangaroos' midfield, and then the Kangaroos would take possession of the ball and start toward the Raiders' goal. But the Raiders would get it back before the Kangaroos could get far. Neither team could get the ball into goal range, and I could tell it was wearing on the players—all that running and hard work but none of the adrenaline rush you get when you're close enough to score. I knew from experience how exhausting that could be!

The teams were evenly matched, and it was hard for either to make a move. Until finally Steven got the ball past one of their defenders and kicked it right past the goalie into the net.

I couldn't help but cheer. "Yes, Steven!"

Jessi rolled her eyes at me, but even if Steven and I didn't agree about the pay issue, I knew he was passionate about soccer and that this championship game meant as much to him as ours did to me. There was no way I couldn't be excited for him.

The Raiders had control of the ball, but Steven managed to steal it away and pass it to Cody, who stopped it with his chest. Two Raiders immediately swarmed him, so he quickly got rid of it, passing it forward to Steven. Then Cody ran up to meet Steven as the Raiders descended around him.

Steven passed the ball to Cody, who tore down the field with it, getting into goal range. He kicked the ball, and the Raiders goalie jumped for it. It brushed against his fingertips before solidly finding the back of the net.

Again I found myself cheering out loud. We were all Kangaroos, and I couldn't help being happy for the boys breaking through that formidable Raiders defense.

Jessi gave an exasperated sigh. "Devin!" she hissed, but I didn't care.

Halftime was called, and we all started looking around eagerly. "Whatever is supposed to happen, it's supposed to happen now," Zoe said, her eyes scanning the field and the bleachers.

"What's it going to be? A marching band? A halftime performance by Beyoncé?" Emma joked.

"Uh-oh," Jessi said as she pointed toward the side of the bleachers. Several of the boys' team players, including Steven and Cody, were wheeling out wagons on either side of the stands. They started passing around colorful balls to everyone sitting there.

"I think those are—" Emma started, but then a kid in the stands took the ball and launched it at someone sitting a few rows behind him.

Splat!

It was a water balloon.

"Have they lost their minds?" Jessi said as, from a dry and safe distance, we watched the pandemonium that ensued.

A teenager tossed a balloon at a group of other teenagers sitting at the top of the stands. Instead of hitting them, it bounced and hit a young girl sitting with her parents. The balloon exploded, drenching her, and she started to cry. Her mother got up angrily and started pointing and yelling at the teenagers.

The stands erupted into chaos. Some of the older kids were laughing, hooting, and hollering, but that soon got drowned out by the angry yelling of the adults.

"Hey, stop that!" a father barked out.

Then we saw Coach Valentine leave the field and approach the stands. When Coach Flores had had to take a leave of absence for a short time when her father had been sick, Coach Valentine had filled in for her as our coach. I'll just say that we were very glad when Coach Flores was back. And I'd never try a stunt like that with him as my coach.

He blew his whistle in front of the stands, and the Kangaroos came running. He yelled and pointed, and soon they were scrambling, trying to get back all the water balloons they'd handed out and put them into the wagons.

I saw one of the refs walk up to Coach Valentine, with the Raiders coach in tow. They moved to the side to talk, and we couldn't hear them, but I saw Coach Valentine gesturing in a very mad way with his hands.

Cody and Steven got back as many balloons as they could. They kept their heads down, and Steven's jersey was soaked.

Coach Valentine blew his whistle again, and all his players lined up. Soon they were running laps around the field, one of his favorite punishments. Steven and Cody passed us but didn't make eye contact. I felt really bad—I wouldn't have known what to say if they had looked our way.

"What were they thinking?" Frida wondered.

Jessi snorted. "They weren't. That's the problem."

Just then a voice came over the loudspeaker. "Today's game will either be rescheduled or decided in favor of the Raiders, once a review has been made by the Gilmore County Middle School Soccer League. We apologize for any inconvenience. Please be careful exiting the bleachers as they may be slippery."

"They were up 2–0 at halftime, and now they might have to forfeit!" Emma exclaimed. "How awful!"

"It serves them right," Jessi said defiantly. "That was such a dumb move. Why did they do that? I thought they said they had something fun planned."

Zoe sighed. "I guess that sounded like fun to them. I don't think they thought it all the way through."

I felt terrible for Steven and Cody and the rest of the team. It had taken so much work to make it to the finals. To blow it all on one bad decision was heartbreaking.

Then another thought came to me. What if one of Brady McCoy's fans showed up and did something crazy?

Would the Kicks be in jeopardy of having to forfeit their finals match too?

CHAPTER TWELVE

On the drive home I stared at my phone, debating whether or not to text Steven—and wondering what to say.

Finally, I typed: I hope the game gets rescheduled. I was rooting for you.

Thanks, he texted back. I'll be rooting for you 2morrow.

That made me feel better. I wasn't sure if Steven and I would stay friends after all of this. It was so complicated. But I'd never ever wanted to see him lose the championship. I genuinely felt bad for him and the whole team, even if it was their fault. I finally admitted to myself that it was a tiny bit unfair that one of our players had a celebrity friend. Who knew what kind of crazy idea we would have come up with to get people to our game if the tables had been turned?

When I got home, I video chatted with Kara and told her the whole story.

"Wow, I can't believe they did that," she replied. "Are you worried that things are going to get out of hand tomorrow, too?"

"I hope not," I said. I took a deep breath. "I feel like there's extra pressure now—not just to fill the stands but to win, you know? Like, we've got everyone watching us, and if we don't have the skills to back up the hype, we're going to look lame."

"Come on, Devin. You *do* have the skills to back it up, and you know it!" Kara said. "Stop psyching yourself out! If I could reach through the screen and shake you, I would."

I laughed. "You're right," I said. "Even if we lose, we're still going to play a strong game."

"You are not going to lose," Kara said.

I rapped my knuckles on my desk. "Knock on wood."

"Don't get superstitious on me now, Devin!" Kara teased. "You got this!"

"Thanks, Kara," I said. She'd made me feel better, and I was able to get some sleep that night.

I woke up the next morning at six, full of energy and nervous excitement. I'm not sure how many times I jogged around the block, because I stopped counting. Mom made me scrambled eggs and oatmeal for breakfast, and then Mom, Dad, Maisie, and I piled into the car and headed for the school.

Coach had asked us to arrive at ten, an hour before the start of the game. Normally when we got to a game field early, the only people hanging around were the kids from each of the teams and their parents.

This morning it was different. The home stands were already starting to fill up!

"There's Juliet and Riley!" Maisie squealed, pointing out the window. "I told you I invited everyone I knew."

"You're the best, Maisie!" I said, and I meant it. How lucky was I to have a little sister who cared about me so much?

"I'm glad we're here with you early," Mom said. "We can beat the crowd and get good seats in the bleachers."

"Yeah," I said as I got out of the car.

Mom and Dad hugged me.

"We are so proud of you, Devin, no matter what happens today," Dad said.

"Thanks!" I said, and I took a deep breath. "I'd better go warm up!"

I jogged up to join my team, and I found Emma trying to calm down a frantic Frida.

"I can't do this!" Frida was saying. "My mind is spinning, and I just can't think straight!"

"What's the matter?" I asked.

Frida pointed to the parking lot. "See that little bus? Miriam brought everyone from the retirement home," she said. "And see those girls over there, with the Brady T-shirts? It worked, Devin! It worked! This game is going to be packed! And I have no idea what character to play out there."

I glanced over at the parking lot and noticed that the Douglas Dragons had just arrived and were getting out of their bus. They looked pretty cool in their green-and-gold uniforms with dragon heads on the front.

"What about a knight defending the castle?" I asked. "Or a princess who kicks butt?"

Frida sighed. "I've done them both already! I need something new for the championship game."

"I know one," Emma said.

"You do?" Frida asked. She grabbed Emma by the arms. "Spit it out! I've got to get into character."

"You should be Frida," Emma said. "Frida Rivera."

"But—" Frida started to object, and Emma interrupted her.

"Frida is a talented soccer player, plus an amazing actor who has had multiple roles on stage and screen," Emma said.

I saw where Emma was going. "Yeah, and she also dresses up like a spy to help out her friends," I added. "She has no fear when she walks into auditions either. Frida is super brave."

"Come on, you guys," Frida said, but I could tell she was loving it. "I can't just go out there and be me. That never works!"

"You've never really given it a try," Emma said. "Just think what a great story this would make. Our hero, who hides under a mask the whole time, in the end reveals her true self to win it all."

Frida's eyes began to shine. "Yeah, I can work with that."

Jessi and Zoe walked up to us.

"Work with what?" Zoe asked. "Did you pick a character for the game?"

"I am Frida Rivera, soccer defender!" Frida said proudly, and she walked away with a dreamy look in her eyes. "I am Frida!"

Jessi raised an eyebrow at me. "Is she okay?"

I nodded. "Better than ever," I said. Then I looked at Zoe. "So . . . is Sabine here?"

Zoe grinned. "Yup. She even gave up a modeling shoot so she could come to the game today."

"Wait, what am I missing here?" Jessi asked.

"Zoe and Sabine like each other," I answered.

"I knew it!" Emma shrieked. "Oh my gosh, you two are the *perfect* couple! You need a couple name. Saboey? Zabine?"

Zoe laughed. "Those are awful!"

Coach blew her whistle, and she started us off with some stretches, and then some squats. I was so pumped for the game, I didn't even feel the burn! Then we did our sock swap, and Emma passed me a blue sock with little green four-leaf clovers on it.

"For luck," Emma said with a grin.

I stood to line up for the game opening, and Foley came over.

"Just so you know, you definitely beat the boys," he said. "We're going to do a complete count, but we're already at more than five hundred people for the girls' game."

I glanced over at the stands, and my jaw dropped. While we'd been warming up, the stands had filled to overflowing. There were people on the sides of the stands, sitting in chairs they'd brought with them; people pressed up against the fence in front of the stands; and still more people coming through the gate!

"Wow!" I said. "That's amazing! Thanks for helping us out with this, Foley."

"You're welcome," he said, and then he looked down at his feet for a second. "So I hope that even when this is all over, we could—"

Foley was interrupted by Coach calling me back to get ready to take the field.

I nodded to Foley and ran to join the team. I wasn't sure what he'd been planning to say, but I couldn't think about that now. It was championship time!

I nervously bounced my foot on the grass. I was jumping out of my skin by the time Mr. Ahmadi, the announcer, called my name and I ran onto the field. This time Grace won the toss, and I took my place with her as a starter, and couldn't wait to get my feet on the ball.

I had my chance when Grace passed it to me. I'd taken it a few feet when one of the Dragons swept up on my right and tried to kick it away. I kicked it to Jessi, and then I ran down the field to see where it would end up.

One of the Dragons intercepted it from Jessi and kicked

it to a teammate, but Megan intercepted it midair with a chest trap and passed it to Grace.

Grace got the ball into goal range, but then the Dragons' defense attacked her like—well, like a horde of dragons! I swear she had three girls covering her, and I had no idea how she was going to get past them.

Then Grace feinted left and moved right quickly. *Just like in practice!* I thought. The defenders stuck close to her, but the move gave her enough room to pass the ball to me.

Then the defenders turned on me. It was intense. Still dribbling, I turned my back on them, looking for someone to pass to, but found nobody open. So I tried one of the practice tips we'd learned and changed my speed, blasting through two defenders. Right before the goal line I slowed down and lobbed the ball high toward the keeper. She jumped up and her right hand touched it, but the ball sailed past her into the net.

"Number thirteen, Devin Burke, scores one point for the Kentville Kicks," Mr. Ahmadi said.

I wasn't prepared for the deafening roar from the crowd, or the chants of "De-vin! De-vin! De-vin!" that happened next. I glanced at the stands and saw Mom, Dad, and Maisie on their feet, cheering me on with everybody else.

Focus, I told myself, and I ran down the field as one of the Dragons took the ball toward our goal zone. She got it all the way up to Frida.

"DE-FENSE! DE-FENSE! DE-FENSE!" the crowd chanted, and Frida glanced over at the crowd, her eyes wide. The Dragons player zipped past her and kicked the ball toward the goal. Emma dove and caught it, landing in the grass.

"Emma, I'm sorry, I failed you!" Frida called out as Emma tossed the ball back into play.

"It's okay!" Emma called back. "Just keep on being Frida!"

We passed the ball down the field, and it ended up with Grace, who used some fancy footwork to get past the defenders again. She sent the ball speeding past the keeper, and we ended the first half up 2–0.

Grace and I high-fived as we lined up for the second quarter. Coach Flores sent Hailey and Zoe in for Giselle and Anjali, and I noticed that the Dragons switched up their goalie.

As the half started, I intercepted a pass between the Dragons and passed the ball to Jessi. She took it downfield and sent a high sideways pass to Grace, who stopped it with her foot. Then the Dragons defenders surrounded her, more determined than before, and within seconds I heard the ref's whistle.

"And it looks like the Dragons are being fouled for pushing," Mr. Ahmadi said. "Kicks player number seven, Grace Kirkland, will get an indirect free kick."

Grace took the kick, and the goalie stopped it. As we jogged back to our side of the field, I asked Grace if she was okay.

"I think it was an accident," she said. "They all came at me pretty hard."

I nodded and watched as the Dragons got control of the ball and maneuvered it to our goal line. Jessi tried to intercept and instead slid on the grass. I helped her up, and we watched as one of the Dragons got past our defense and kicked the ball low and to the side of the net—and scored.

Emma's face fell.

"That's okay, we got this!" I called out to her, and I vowed to score another goal before the second quarter. After some back-and-forth on both sides, Jessi headed the ball to me. I stopped it with my foot and took it to the Dragons' goal.

Two Dragons defenders charged toward me so fast, I had no time to think. I changed direction and ran right into the elbow of a third defender. The collision knocked the wind out of me and left me flat on my back on the field.

I heard the ref's whistle, and I tried to get up, but the blow had left me stunned. The next thing I knew, hands were pulling me up and Coach ran out onto the field.

"You okay, Devin?" she asked.

"I . . . I'm okay," I insisted.

"Just sit out for a little bit, okay?" she suggested.

I didn't argue. Megan ran in to replace me, and I sat on the bench. Mom was already there.

"Devin, how do you feel?" she asked worriedly. "Did you black out? Can you breathe?"

"I'm fine, Mom," I assured her. "I just got hit hard. I want to go back in and play."

Mom nodded to the ambulance parked by the entrance. "Let's just get you checked out first."

Now, I was used to sitting out part of the game so everyone would get a chance to play. But it was the championship game. I didn't want to sit out now!

I knew I couldn't argue with Mom, though. I followed her to the ambulance, and two EMTs checked my heart with a stethoscope, and even checked my blood pressure. Outside, I could hear the Dragons cheering. They'd scored again, tying up the game 2–2.

By now my knee was bouncing up and down a mile a minute, and one of the EMTs laughed.

"I think she's going to be good to play," he said.

"Thanks so much," Mom said, and I sprinted out of the ambulance and back to the Kicks sideline.

It was halftime, and Coach was gathering the team for a pep talk. The mood was pretty tense.

"I just don't know how to get past them," Grace was saying.

"This whole 'being Frida' thing isn't working," Frida said.

"I think I'm off my game today," Emma said.

"I know how you feel," I admitted. As eager as I was to get back into the game, that collision had shaken me.

"Do not lose confidence, girls!" Coach Flores said. "You had great momentum when the game started. You can do that again. Look for openings. I want to see you passing."

"Yes, Coach!" we yelled.

Coach put me back in to start the second half, with Megan, Zoe, Hailey, Jessi, and Taylor on offense. I started the game off with a pass to Megan, and we made our way down the field. Megan passed to Zoe, who zigzagged across the field and passed to Jessi. Then she passed the ball to Hailey, and Hailey passed it to me. Once again the Dragons defenders surrounded me, and I got the ball back to Hailey quickly, before they could get too close. Hailey tried to score, but the keeper caught it.

"Keep doing what you're doing!" Coach called out, and I waited for my next offensive opportunity as the Dragons took the ball toward our goal. When they got close, Frida charged toward the Dragon with the ball.

"I'm ready for my close-up!" she yelled, and she kicked the ball away from the Dragon. Giselle got it and passed it to Taylor, and we kept up our passing game until I was in goal range. I was about to shoot when two defenders started to close in on me, and I panicked and passed it to Jessi. One of the Dragons intercepted the pass.

I cringed. I could have had that goal shot! I *should* have had it.

The Dragons sent the ball out-of-bounds, and before the throw-in, Coach called for a time-out.

"Devin, I'm sending Grace back in!" Coach called.

I was surprised. Coach had never pulled me out in the middle of a half before. I jogged back to the bench.

"I swear, I'm feeling fine, Coach," I said.

"It's not that," Coach said. "That bang-up has got you a little cautious, that's all. Hang out and get your head together."

Cautious? I guessed Coach was talking about how I had stopped trying to get through the defenders. I sat down on the bench next to Emma, who was sitting out while Zarine took the goal, and I watched the game. Pretty quickly Grace got the ball back into the goal zone. One defender approached from the left, and one approached from the right. Grace saw the one on the left but didn't notice the other player. The Dragon on the right intercepted the ball.

I kept watching. Jessi got the ball back and passed it to Zoe, who had the fastest footwork on our team. She zipped right past the defenders and shot for the goal, but another Dragon raced in front of her and kicked the ball out-of-bounds.

The Dragons got control of the ball right after that, and one of their players took it all the way down the field and shot it into the goal, past Zarine.

I looked at Emma, and she was shaken. Now the Dragons had a one-point lead.

The third quarter ended with the Dragons still up by one. Coach brought us in for one last huddle.

"Don't let this get you down," she said. "I know you, and I know you have it in you to bring this game home. I've seen you do it before."

Behind her the crowd had launched into a chant. "Go, Kicks! Go, Kicks! Kicks! Kicks! Kicks!"

Coach smiled. "Hear that? Feel that energy? That's for you. You created this. Now use it! Bring it with you onto the field!"

"Coach is right!" I cried. "We can do this!"

We put our hands together and joined the crowd. "Go, Kicks! Go, Kicks! Kicks, Kicks, KICKS!"

I looked at Coach. "Please put me in. I got this!"

Coach nodded. "I know you do. All right, Devin. You're in for Hailey."

As I ran onto the field, I put everything out of my head. I wasn't thinking about Steven or Foley. I wasn't thinking about getting flattened by that Dragons defender. I wasn't thinking about news reporters or celebrity tweets or even #EqualPay.

All I was thinking about was that soccer ball.

The Dragons started passing the ball down the field. Jessi intercepted it midfield and brought it into Dragons territory. She passed it to me, and I saw two defenders coming from either side. They were on me pretty quickly.

I didn't panic. I didn't ditch the ball. Instead, I automatically dribbled to the right, stepped over the ball with my right foot, and then kicked it into the open space away from me with my left. The defenders moved right, and I caught up to the ball and took it to the goal line.

Bam! I kicked the ball so hard that for a second I

thought it was going to pop. Instead it rocketed past the keeper into the net.

"Whoo!" I cheered, my heart pounding. Without thinking, I'd used the scissor feint from practice, and it had worked!

"Devin Burke scores again, evening up the score 3–3," Mr. Ahmadi said.

It felt good to tie up the game, but I wanted to do more.

I wanted to win.

I raced around that field like I was on fire. I made two more goal attempts that their keeper stopped. Emma was back on goal, and she stopped one goal attempt made by the Dragons. It was the only one, because Frida and the defenders didn't let anyone else get close.

As the clock ticked down, the fans got louder and louder.

"Kicks! Kicks! KICKS! KICKS!"

I glanced at the clock. Thirty seconds left. We'd be going into overtime for sure.

Then Frida stopped a Dragon's goal attempt by getting in front of it and kicking the ball to midfield. Jessi got it and passed it to Zoe. One of the Dragons swooped in and intercepted, and then kicked it high and sideways to one of her teammates. I jumped up and headed the ball to Zoe. She zipped past the Dragons' startled defense and kicked it into the Dragons' goal.

"Did you see that play?" Mr. Ahmadi asked. "Kicks number thirteen, Devin Burke, intercepts and passes to number twelve, Zoe Quinlan, who makes the goal."

The final whistle blew.

"Kicks win the Division Thirty-Four State Championship!"

The Kicks stands erupted in cheers. My teammates flew off the bench, and every one of us crushed together in a huddle, jumping up and down and screaming. Then we broke up to shake hands with the Dragons. I felt for them, I really did. But I was so happy we'd won!

After the last handshake, Frida, Zoe, Emma, Jessi, and I practically tackled one another in our joy.

"I can't believe it," Emma said. "Last fall the Kicks were one of the worst teams in the league. And now look at us."

"We're the best!" Frida shrieked.

Jessi wrapped me in a choke hold. "It's because of Devin! She came from Connecticut and saved us!"

"Are you kidding? You guys saved me," I said. "I was all alone when I came here, with no friends. And then I found you. We make a great team."

Zoe smiled. "The best team."

When we got to the sideline, the TV news cameras were back. Mom walked up to me.

"Devin, the reporter would like to talk to you, and I said it's okay, if it's okay with you," she said.

"Sure," I said, and I was too pumped up with adrenaline to feel nervous. The reporter wore a blue blazer and had shiny brown hair in waves all around her face.

"Devin Burke, I understand that this competition to

get fans into the stands was your idea," she said. "Do you think you proved that the boys were wrong?"

"What we proved is that girls can play just as hard and just as well as boys," I said. "And we can pack the stands just like boys can."

"You certainly did," the reporter said. "Congratulations on winning the championship. You had some great moves out there. Do you think you'll go pro someday?"

At that moment a feeling washed over me that I'll never forget. It was a feeling down deep in my heart, in my bones, that I knew I was going to play soccer for the rest of my life. I was going to keep working hard at it until I became the best that I could be. And I was going to go pro. I could almost see a vision of myself in a huge arena, filled with cheering fans.

"Yes!" I answered her. "Maybe one day you'll be interviewing me after the women's team wins the World Cup!"

The reporter laughed. "That would be great for both of us," she said. "Thanks, Devin."

I jogged back to my friends. Zoe and Sabine were hugging and jumping up and down.

"Sabine!" I called out. "Thanks for coming!"

"Of course," she said. Then she flashed her model smile and motioned to her T-shirt. "I even wore Kicks blue!"

Then I felt a tap on my shoulder and turned around. It was Steven! Cody and some of the other boys from the team were behind him.

"You guys came!" I cried.

"Congratulations on the championship!" Steven said. He held out his hand. "And congratulations on beating us. You won fair and square."

"Well, maybe the fact that we knew a celebrity was a little unfair," I said. "Are you going to be able to play the Raiders again? Or did they win by forfeit?"

"Looks like we're playing next Saturday," Steven replied. "The league director went easy on us because of the 'stress' of our bet with you, or something like that." He shrugged.

That sort of sounded like the league was blaming us for the boys' mistake, but we didn't have anything more to prove to them, so I didn't let it bother me. Besides, I wanted the boys to have a second chance, and they had to win on their own.

"Awesome! I hope you win," I said.

Steven smiled. "Do you want to go to the mall? Maybe the arcade?"

"No thanks," I replied, and I surprised myself with how quickly I'd come up with the answer. I motioned toward my teammates. "I'm pretty sure we're going to go celebrate."

"Maybe next weekend, then," Steven said.

"Maybe," I replied, and then I spied Foley's cute freckled face on the edge of the crowd of people around the team, waiting to get in. "Later, Steven!"

I made my way to Foley, and he broke into a huge smile when he saw me.

"Devin, you did it!" he cried. "Congratulations!"

"Thanks!" I said. "I still can't believe it."

He pushed a strand of hair away from his eyes. "I know you're probably going out with the team, but maybe later we could meet up for some ice cream?"

I grinned. "Yeah, I'd like that," I said. "I'll text you."

"Great," Foley said, and then he gave me a shy wave and walked away.

Jessi ran up and grabbed me by the arm.

"Emma's mom's driving! We're going to celebrate," she said, and she practically dragged me toward Emma, Zoe, and Frida. As we flew across the field, an image flashed into my mind.

I saw myself, older, wearing a red-white-and-blue uniform. My sun-streaked hair streamed behind me as I dribbled a soccer ball. In the stadium around me, thousands of people filled the stands, and they cheered me on with a deafening roar.

"Earth to Devin!"

Jessi's voice roused me from my vision. I realized I was standing in the grass, staring up at the sky. My friends were all giving me strange looks.

"Did that run-in with the Dragons defender scramble her brain?" Emma asked.

"I just auditioned for a movie about a girl who gets hit in the head and thinks she's someone else," Frida said. "Maybe I should study you for research, Devin."

"Devin's fine!" Zoe said.

"And she'll be finer after we get some pizza into her,"

Jessi said, grabbing my arm again. "Into the van, superstar!"

The image in my head slowly faded as I climbed into the van behind my friends. Had I just seen a glimpse of my real future as a pro soccer player?

That would be amazing. But the future was a long way away. And right now I had everything I needed—family and friends who loved me, and a great soccer team.

I had the Kicks, and no matter where else I went in life, the Kicks would always be with me.